A Frightening Fangs-giving

Country Cottage Mystery #11

Addison Moore

and

Bellamy Bloom

Edited by Paige Maroney Smith
Cover by Lou Harper, Cover Affairs
Published by Hollis Thatcher Press, LTD.

Copyright © 2020 by Addison Moore, Bellamy Bloom

This novel is a work of fiction. Any resemblance to peoples either living or deceased is purely coincidental. Names, places, and characters are figments of the author's imagination. The author holds all rights to this work. It is illegal to reproduce this novel without written expressed consent from the author herself.

All Rights Reserved.

Books by the Authors

Cozy Mysteries

Country Cottage Mysteries

Kittyzen's Arrest (Country Cottage Mysteries 1)
Dog Days of Murder (Country Cottage Mysteries 2)
Santa Claws Calamity (Country Cottage Mysteries 3)
Bow Wow Big House (Country Cottage Mysteries 4)
Murder Bites (Country Cottage Mysteries 5)
Felines and Fatalities (Country Cottage Mysteries 6)
A Killer Tail (Country Cottage Mysteries 7)
Cat Scratch Cleaver (Country Cottage Mysteries 8)
Just Buried (Country Cottage Mysteries 9)
Butchered After Bark (Country Cottage Mysteries 10)
A Frightening Fangs-giving (Country Cottage Mysteries 11)
A Christmas to Dismember (Country Cottage Mysteries 12)
Sealed with a Hiss (Country Cottage Mysteries 13)

Meow for Murder

An Awful Cat-titude (Meow for Murder #1)
A Dreadful Meow-ment (Meow for Murder 2)
A Claw-some Affair (Meow for Murder 3)
A Haunted Hallow-whiskers (Meow for Murder 4)

A Candy Cane Cat-astrophe (Meow for Murder 5)

Murder in the Mix

Cutie Pies and Deadly Lies (Murder in the Mix 1)
Bobbing for Bodies (Murder in the Mix 2)
Pumpkin Spice Sacrifice (Murder in the Mix 3)
Gingerbread and Deadly Dread (Murder in the Mix 4) Seven-Layer Slayer (Murder in the Mix 5)
Red Velvet Vengeance (Murder in the Mix 6)
Bloodbaths and Banana Cake (Murder in the Mix 7)
New York Cheesecake Chaos (Murder in the Mix 8)
Lethal Lemon Bars (Murder in the Mix 9)
Macaron Massacre (Murder in the Mix 10)
Wedding Cake Carnage (Murder in the Mix 11)
Donut Disaster (Murder in the Mix 12)
Toxic Apple Turnovers (Murder in the Mix 13)
Killer Cupcakes (Murder in the Mix 14)
Pumpkin Pie Parting (Murder in the Mix 15)
Yule Log Eulogy (Murder in the Mix 16)
Pancake Panic (Murder in the Mix 17)
Sugar Cookie Slaughter (Murder in the Mix 18)
Devil's Food Cake Doom (Murder in the Mix 19)
Snickerdoodle Secrets (Murder in the Mix 20)
Strawberry Shortcake Sins (Murder in the Mix 21)
Cake Pop Casualties (Murder in the Mix 22)

Flag Cake Felonies (Murder in the Mix 23)
Peach Cobbler Confessions (Murder in the Mix 24)
Poison Apple Crisp (Murder in the Mix 25) Spooky Spice Cake Curse (Murder in the Mix #26)
Pecan Pie Predicament (Murder in the Mix 27)
Eggnog Trifle Trouble (Murder in the Mix 28)

1

Two hours from now...

"Donuts! Thank you." I snap up a handful of the mini apple cider creations and gulp them down. "Donuts have always been my downfall." I glower at the beast in front of me. "Why are you looking at me like that?"

"I just want you to be happy. And if these donuts make you happy, by all means have as many as you want."

"You don't have to tell me twice," I say, taking another handful. "You know, for someone whose life I've worked to make a living hell, you are being awfully nice to me today. What do you want?" I give a little wink when I say it. "I've always been in the driver's seat in this relationship, and no matter what you're up to, I always will be."

"Who cares what I want. It's all about what you want, isn't it?"

"You're not wrong. And don't you forget it. This day, this life is all about me. How does it make you feel that I practically *own* you?" A laugh quivers through me, but my throat closes off and it can't quite initiate. "I think I need some air."

"Let's step outside."

We head for the back of my shop and I speed into the alley where the icy autumn air cools me instantly, but I can't seem to catch my breath.

The sound of kittens mewling catches my attention, and I spot three small cats in a plain brown box yipping and squirming.

I try to take a step in their direction, but I end up staggering to keep from falling.

"Something's wrong." I claw at my neck as my vision blurs and my throat catches fire. "Help me." I turn to the creature next to me. "Don't just stand there. Call for help. I can't breathe."

"You can't breathe, can you? And soon you'll have taken your last breath. I heard you threatening to haunt someone a few minutes ago. Now you'll have your chance. Don't ever say I didn't do anything for you. But then again, in less than a few minutes, you won't ever say anything again. Goodbye. Sleep tight. You certainly won't be missed by anyone—least of all not me."

"You did this?" My voice comes out in less than a whisper.

My knees give way as I fall hard to the ground. Those cruel eyes, that ghastly grimace watching from above is the last thing I see.

"Happy haunting," are the last words I hear.

The present...

"I'm going to kill her."

"I wouldn't say those words in Cider Cove," I say to my sister while we both stare out at the melee across the street. Macy and I are standing right outside of her soap and candle shop, Lather and Light, while witnessing the unveiling of a brand-new business, directly across from hers, who just revealed their signage and opened their doors to an entire herd of enthused customers. The name of the shop in question just so happens to be Suds and Illuminations, and if the name suggests anything, my guess is that my sister is very much going to be capable of a homicide by the end of this day.

My sister's quaint little shop has been a staple here in Cider Cove for years. It's light and bright inside with its buy-one-get-one-free candle display that hits you as soon as you step inside, and there's even a large wisteria tree with lavender leaves set in her window. Every branch is wrapped in twinkle lights, and it gives off a homey yet enchanted feel.

I can't imagine what Ember Sweet was thinking when she decided to open up a shop right across the street, selling the exact same products with a near identical name.

It's a windblown November in our little corner of Maine, and it just so happens to be the one-hundredth birthday of our cozy little town. All of Cider Cove has gathered right here on Main Street to celebrate the kickoff to the Founders' Day Festival, a month-long extravaganza that will culminate on Thanksgiving Day with a parade that boasts to rival anything New York has to offer. There will be festivals and celebrations going on all over Cider Cove throughout the month. And the cozy little inn I run happens to be playing host to the official Founders' Day concert in a little over a week.

Sugar Shack, a huge country band, is set to perform down at the cove that butts up to the inn, and even though I'm responsible for overseeing the event, I'm just as excited as any groupie.

My name is Bizzy Baker, and I can read minds. Wait, let's do that again. My name is Bizzy Baker *Wilder*, and I can read minds. Not every mind, not every time, but it happens, and believe me when I say, it's not all it's cracked up to be. Like now for instance.

Of course, Bizzy doesn't want me to say those words out loud. My sister muses while scowling at the shop that's threatening to take down her business. ***Once Ember's body turns up, she'll be forced to turn me over to the sheriff's department. Lord knows the entire town has lost count of how many corpses she's stumbled across in the last year alone. She's practically a corpse magnet. I won't need an alibi when I off Ember. I'll have my trusty little sis to take the heat for me.***

I pull my sister close by the arm, our eyes still glued to the heresy playing out. The scent of sugary baked goods enlivens my senses, as just about every food vendor in town is hocking their wares out in the streets today. The inn is giving away complimentary apple cider mini donuts down by the gazebo in Town Square, and my stomach is growling just thinking about them.

"Come on, Macy. You grew up with Ember. We should go say hello. And look, Georgie and Juni are already there." I bet they're not contemplating murder either.

"Because they're traitors." She doesn't miss a beat.

Macy and I do our best to navigate the thick crowd while Fish, my sweet long-haired black and white tabby, sits in the tote bag I've cinched to my shoulders with her cute little head poking out as to not miss any of the action. I've got my dog,

Sherlock Bones, on a leash, and he's just as anxious to get through the crowd as we are. Sherlock has the most expressive button brown eyes and smiling face. He's a red and white freckled mixed breed that actually belonged to my husband first.

My *husband*—those words still sound like a dream. Jasper Wilder and I tied the knot back in September, and we've yet to come down off cloud nine. Nor do we plan to. He's still finishing up at work, but should be joining us at any minute. And after what Macy and I just witnessed, it can't be soon enough.

Jasper is the lead homicide detective at the Seaview Sheriff's Department, and if my sister gets her way, there will most certainly be a homicide today.

Don't get me wrong. Macy Baker is no killer. If anything, she's always been far more cosmopolitan than Cider Cove allows. We're both in our late twenties. We share the same dark hair and denim blue eyes, but she's taken to dyeing her locks a severe shade of platinum. She's donned a black leather jacket and dark jeans, which are artfully yet nonsensically shredded, along with a pair of cute leather boots. The entire outfit is essentially her uniform, everyone knows that. But I'll admit, those boots had me wincing once I saw them. The boots themselves are lovely. It's the five-inch heels that had me cringing. They look far too torturous to wear on any given day, let alone this one where walking up and down Main Street is practically required.

But Macy has never been practical, as evidenced by her inch and a half long acrylic nails. They're painted a glittery shade of amber that shimmers when it catches the light. And they add the perfect decorative touch for fall.

In fact, the entire town has been decorated for fall, with its thick strings of silk autumn leaves and tiny orange twinkle lights that run along Main Street, giving our sweet coastal paradise a magical appeal. Fall is my favorite time of year, with its plethora of pumpkins, the apple cider, the leaves changing colors—not to mention the cozy coats and boots I can finally mix into my wardrobe. And this year, the Founders' Day Festival was something I was particularly looking forward to, right up until this moment.

Fish jabs me in the chest with her paw. ***She's not really going to kill someone, is she, Bizzy?***

Yes, I can read the minds of animals, too. And believe me, I often prefer their thoughts to that of humans. Both Fish and Sherlock Bones know that I can understand them, and somehow they seem to understand each other, too. Only a handful of people know about my strange ability, but my sister isn't one of them. Not that we're not close, it's just that some horrible secrets are better kept hidden in order to avoid unnecessary family drama and potentially lengthy stays in psychiatric hospitals.

Sherlock lets out a sharp bark. *If Macy does the girl in, the case will be easy to solve. But we're not really going to turn Macy in, are we? I'm sorry if it ruins your track record. But for the sake of family unity, I say we let this one slide, Biz.*

I shake my head over at Sherlock as if to answer his question. But he's not wrong. I've got a track record, all right, for both stumbling upon a body and hunting down the killer. I guess you can say getting wrapped up in a homicide investigation is my second odd quirk. But that odd quirk happens to be how I met my gorgeous husband, so I've chosen to overlook the murderous patina and embrace it as my strange gift.

"Bizzy Baker *Wilder*!" Georgie Conner, an eighty-something gloriously happy hippie whom I consider to be family, waves me over in her direction where she stands wearing an orange kaftan as bright as a traffic cone. "Guess what?" she chirps. "I've got the hot new shop in town to agree to sell a few of my quilts!"

"That's wonderful!" I grin at the news, right up until I realize she's talking about the questionable shop that just opened.

Georgie has gray wiry hair that sits at her shoulders, and her eyes are baby blue with just enough mischief in each one to let you know she means business. And standing beside her is her daughter, Juniper Moonbeam, better known as Juni.

Juni is basically Georgie minus a few gray hairs and wrinkles—and a little more rock and roll biker chick and a lot less happy hippie. Fun fact: Juni was once briefly married to my father. I can't remember if she was wife number three or thirteen. My father goes through wives like some people go through a bag of chips.

I'm a bit prideful to say my mother was the first Mrs. Baker, and she lived to tell the tale—or more to the point, she let *him* live to tell the tale. They're both wonderful parents, just not while joined in holy matrimony to each other.

A horrible groan comes from my sister. "Georgie!" she snips. "How dare you sell your crooked quilts at that copycat establishment."

Georgie grunts, "They're called *wonky* quilts. And when I offered to sell them at your place, you told me to take my bohemian blankets and hit the highway."

The wonky quilts are a rather new hobby of hers. Georgie is actually a mosaic artist who specializes in the use of sea glass. But last month after the inn hosted a haunted quilt display—long, horrible story—she basically fell in love with the idea of creating artful bedding. It's safe to say Georgie has put her artistic spin on these quilts, with their large swaths of fabric pieced every which way and unfinished edges that give them a fringed look. They're mostly made up of bright random patterns, but the ones she's been working on lately all seem to have an autumn theme to them with pumpkins and maple leaves in every color.

Macy nods with an incredulous look on her face. "And when I told you to hit the highway, I said it with love."

Juni snorts as she wraps herself in one of Georgie's wonky quilts, a black and orange design with fall leaves printed all over it. "That's right, Macy. And then you told her to try her luck somewhere where they might actually buy into daydreams and delusions—and she did. If my mama is anything, she's tenacious. And now look? The shop has been open for less than a half hour and she's already sold *three*!"

Macy scowls. "That's because you probably bought them all."

"I bought one because it happened to be freezing out." Juni cinches the quilt tightly around herself before smacking her mother on the shoulder. "I just had a brilliant idea! Three words—wonky quilt *jacket*!"

"*Yes!*" Georgie howls so loud you'd think she won the lottery. "I'll get right on those, Toots. Oh, we are going to make a killing off of them."

The crowd thins and we can see clearly into Suds and Illuminations, causing both Macy and me to gasp at the very same time.

Much like my sister's quaint shop, this overnight pop-up has the same buy-one-get-one-free candle display at the front of the store. And sitting in the window is a large lavender wisteria tree strewn with twinkle lights almost identical to the one my sister has.

A petite blonde steps out of the establishment in question and sheds an easy smile our way.

"Well, if it isn't two of my favorite people, the Baker sisters!" ***It's showtime! Let's see how fast I can push all of Macy Baker's buttons. Here's hoping for a nuclear explosion on her part.***

She lets out a howl of delight, and before we know it, she's accosting both Macy and me with an enthusiastic embrace.

Ember Sweet was one of Macy's best friends way back in junior high. But they had a falling-out and things were never the same. Ember moved away from Cider Cove for a while, but now she's back—looking staggeringly like my sister with her short blonde bob, not to mention the replica of my sister's long established business.

Ember has a pretty face, full fuchsia lips and tiny turned up nose. And she happens to be wearing my sister's signature black leather jacket, trendy jeans, and boots. The younger version of Ember Sweet that I remember had stringy *brown* hair, and there is definitely something off-putting about the way she seems to have crafted herself into my sister's likeness. Obviously, something nefarious is going on here. Why else would she open up a shop directly across the street from my sister, with the exact same inventory more or less, and show up looking like a living replica?

Before my sister can get a single aggressive and rather *salty* word out—and believe me, Macy has an entire cache of salty words in her lexicon—a couple pops up next to us, and I don't know whether to smile or frown at the two of them.

"Mayor Woods," I say as I inspect my longtime nemesis. "Hux." I pull my brother into a quick embrace.

"Bizzy." Mackenzie offers an indifferent shrug my way.

Mackenzie Woods is basically my Ember Sweet.

Mack and I were good friends growing up—right up until she pushed me into a whiskey barrel and landed me in the supernatural predicament I'm in to begin with. After nearly drowning, I decided I no longer cared for confined spaces, bodies of water, or Mack Woods.

But I let my friendship with Mack drag on for a few more years until she decided that stealing every one of my boyfriends was her new favorite hobby. And the biggest takeaway from the not-so-friendly shove? I came away with the ability to pry into other people's minds. It turns out, I'm something called transmundane, further classified as telesensual, which basically means I can read minds.

Hux leans my way. "Why is Macy growling like an attack dog ready to pounce?"

I make a face at my brother. He shares my dark hair and light eyes and happens to be a top-notch divorce attorney—a career he'll need to lean on if he ever plans on taking things to a matrimonial level with the piranha he's leashed himself to. I'm not thrilled with the fact he's gotten serious with Mackenzie Woods, of all people.

"Take a look around," I whisper, and Hux does a quick evaluation of the signage before his eyes bug out. "Exactly."

Ember pulls Mackenzie in by the hand. "Everyone!" she shouts to the crowd of women all bustling their way into her store. "Mayor Woods was kind enough to agree to christen my little shop on this, the one hundredth birthday, of this fabulous town."

Mackenzie stuns in a navy power suit and a matching dark trench coat on over that. She has a shock of long chestnut hair and large amber eyes that give off just enough wickedness to warn others to keep at an emotional arm's length. Apparently, my brother isn't interested in heeding the warning.

"Hear ye, hear ye"—Mackenzie laughs as a thicket of bodies gather around—"I'd like to be the very first to welcome this fine establishment to the town of Cider Cove!"

Another blonde emerges from the store, who oddly enough also looks like a Macy Baker knockoff. I'm sensing a disturbing theme here. She's dressed in the same dark leather jacket, shredded jeans, and boots. And in her hand she wields a bottle of champagne.

Ember snatches the bubbly from her. "Has this been chilled?"

The blonde gives a frenetic nod. *As chilly as your black heart.*

I can't help but hold back a smile at the quip. I learned long ago not to judge anyone for whatever they might be thinking.

Next to the blonde is a tall brunette with shoulder-length hair and icy green eyes.

She takes a breath as she looks over at Ember. *All right, you little brat, let's get this over with so I can go stuff my face with whatever that sugary scent is that will find its way into my stomach soon enough. I've got a lot on the agenda this afternoon, and I'm going to need to keep up my energy.*

The woman has sharp features, thin cranberry painted lips, and an overall look of indifference to the setting around her. I'd say she has a couple of years on Ember, and so far I'm liking her best. What can I say? My stomach is itching for whatever that sugary scent is, too.

Ember lifts her chin. "Thank you, Mayor Woods, for welcoming both my business partner, Willow Taylor, and me." She pulls the blonde in close and they look like sisters. "We are so very privileged to be a part of the Cider Cove community, and we look forward to many successful years, right here on Main Street!" She sets down a knee-high wooden sign that has the shop's name on it and creates a small clearing as she hands the bottle of champagne over to Mackenzie.

It takes less than a tap for the bottle to crack and champagne to bubble and ooze down the sign as the crowd grows wild with cheers.

Mackenzie waves to the thicket of people. "Now if you'll all join me at the gazebo at the end of the street, we'll kick off the Founders' Day Festival and get this party started! The Country Cottage Café has donated enough apple cider donuts to feed the entire seaboard. This is going to be a great month and a great one hundredth year for all of Cider Cove!"

She leashes her arm through my brother's as they stride toward the gazebo that's festooned with fall leaves and pumpkins. The high school band is tuning up, and there's a giant arch made of balloons that hovers over an expansive banner strung over the gazebo. The banner reads *Welcome to the Founders' Day Festival! Happy Birthday, Cider Cove! One hundred years and counting!*

"Congratulations," I say to Ember, much to the horror of my sister. "It's nice to see you again." I'm not thrilled about what she's done, but I'm not committed to helping my sister hide the body either.

Bizzy! Fish yowls from the tote bag warming my side. ***If you're not careful, Macy might just want to kill you, too.***

Sherlock barks. ***She's not wrong.***

She's not, but that's beside the point.

"Bizzy Baker." Ember's eyes light up like blue flames. "Look at you! You've grown up to be a beautiful young woman."

My lips twitch because it just so happens that Ember, much like my sister, is just one year older than me.

"Thank you," I tell her.

"What are you doing now? How have you been?"

Macy grunts as she rolls her eyes my way, ***Careful, Bizzy. She just might be gunning to replicate your life next.***

"I happen to run the Country Cottage Inn just down the street. And I just got married in September, so I'm Mrs. Baker Wilder now."

"Oh, isn't that nice." She takes up my left hand and her thumb dances over my wedding ring. ***Bizzy deserves to be happy. I hope her happiness makes Macy all that much more miserable.***

Miserable? Boy, she's really got it out for her. Not that my saucy sister hasn't amassed her fair share of enemies over the years, but this seems to be a bit over the top.

"And what a stunner this is," she muses as she inspects my wedding ring at close range.

It's true, my wedding ring is a stunner, with its emerald cut diamond encrusted with smaller diamonds that drip down the sides. I'm in love with it almost as much as I am with Jasper.

Ember shoots a curt look to my sister. "And you, Macy? Let me guess, you're far too cagey to let any man hold you down." ***I know it for a fact. And don't think I'm going to let you off the hook with your man-eating ways either. I'm here to grind you down and make you ten times as miserable as you've made me.***

My eyes bulge upon hearing her heated thoughts.

Good Lord, what has my sister done now? It's not a secret that Macy Baker is no saint. But is she really that bad of a sinner?

Macy sheds a sour smile. "Why, I'm happily single, Ember, thank you for asking. Now if you'll excuse me, I have a well-established and much-loved business to tend to." She clears her throat. "Fifty percent off all candles over at Lather and Light!"

Macy zips across the street, and a small stampede follows along with her.

Ember glowers in my sister's direction, and a cold chill runs through me just looking at the sight.

You will rue the day you ever thought to mess with me, Macy Baker. I'm taking you down or I'll die trying. Rumor has it, there has been a string of murders in Cider Cove. A tiny smile twitches on her lips. ***Pity if Macy's body should turn up next.***

A breath catches in my throat as I pull Fish close.

Ember forces a smile as she cups her hands around her mouth. "Seventy-five percent off all candles! Today only!"

Georgie and Juni join in on the feeding frenzy as half of Main Street vacuums into the small little shop.

It looks as if Macy had better watch her back.

And if Ember is smart, she had better watch hers, too.

My sister doesn't take well to being challenged in any capacity. Something tells me neither does Ember.

Let's just hope a body doesn't turn up before the day is through.

A wild wind picks up and blows the leaves over the crowd as if they were confetti.

A FRIGHTENING FANGS-GIVING

Brace yourself. My mind picks up on the strange voice, and I can't tell where it's coming from or if it's from a man or a woman. Often, if the mind I'm inadvertently prying into isn't within my visual range, the voice comes across as a bit androgynous.

You'll pay for what you've done to me. Enjoy yourself while you can. I can promise—this will be the last day of your life.

I gasp as I spin and take in the crowd.

An autumn chill is in the air, and so is murder.

2

The wind blows in from the navy Atlantic and sends an icy chill up my spine as I look up and down Main Street at the throngs of bundled bodies all heading toward the gazebo like salmon swimming upstream. In the exact opposite direction, at the other end of this bustling road, sits the Country Cottage Inn, the place I've been managing for the last six years. The owner is a wealthy earl from England named Quinn Bennet who lets me have full run of the place while he pays the bills. It's a match made in employment heaven and I wouldn't want it any other way.

But right now Fish, Sherlock, and I have drifted from that knockoff shop of my sister's as we migrate our way down the road until I come upon two familiar, and by the looks of it, happy to see me faces—both of which happen to be holding a platter of apple cider mini donuts dusted with powdered sugar.

"Emmie!" I hop over and pull my bestie into a quick embrace.

Emmie Crosby and I share the same long dark hair, light eyes, and penchant for trouble. We've been locked at the best friend hip for as long as I can remember. Not only do we look alike, but we share the same first name, Elizabeth. So in an effort to avoid confusion, we've gone through life using our nicknames and have never looked back at our formal monikers.

"Hey, Bizzy." Leo Granger glides an arm around Emmie's waist.

Leo is a tall, dark-haired, dark-eyed, handsome stud who happens to be my husband's best friend. They had a falling-out ages ago that concerned a woman, but they've recently moved past it just in time to have Leo as the best man at our wedding. And it just so happens that Leo shares my strange little mind reading quirk—it's how we met about a year ago. And as of just last week, Emmie is in on our mind reading secret as well.

Emmie leans in, her eyes growing wide as she bites down on a smile. *Have a donut, Bizzy. They're delicious.* Emmie is in charge of the kitchen at the Country Cottage Café, and her specialty just so happens to be baking tasty treats like this one. **Wink once if you love it.**

"I have no doubt I will," I say, giving her a wink regardless as I snap one up. "*Mmm!*" I moan through a bite.

Emmie bursts out with a laugh. "I can't get over this. How could you hold out on me for so long, Bizzy? Think of all the fun we could have had. I could have told you secrets right out in the open. Think of all the tests and quizzes I could have helped you out with. And don't get me started on the crude jokes I could have been spewing while you were giving your valedictory speech."

A laugh bumps through me. "I'm just glad you're still speaking to me."

Honestly, I didn't know how Emmie was going to take the news that I was keeping something so supernaturally bizarre from her. But thankfully, she took it all in stride.

Sherlock lets out a bark. **Hand one of those donuts over, Bizzy! One won't kill me. And I promised Jasper I'd protect you. They could be poison.**

Leo is quick to toss one over to him. "There you go, buddy. They're not poison, but they are addictive."

Sherlock barks once again. **They're just as good as bacon! Another, please!**

And, of course, Leo is quick to comply. He can't help it. Leo is not only a good guy, he's a dog lover by nature.

Emmie bumps her shoulder to mine. "So what do you think of all the chaos?" she asks, glancing around at the festivities. "I've already pointed about a dozen people over to the café. This is going to be great for business."

"For every business." Leo pops an apple cider donut into his own mouth, too. *Especially the private business I get to conduct with this little cutie later.* He pulls Emmie in close with a drugged smile on his face.

Smooth, Romeo, I quip and he shoots me a quick look.

Sorry, Biz. I can't help it. My mind tends to wander when I'm around her, and it tends to forget you can pry right into it.

"Anyway"—I shed a quick wink his way—"this might be good for some businesses but definitely not Macy's." I give them a quick rundown on Suds and Illuminations, and the two of them stare off at the shop with their mouths open.

"Wow." Emmie ticks her head. "That is one brave girl. Macy is going to eviscerate her."

"Speaking of which." I'm just about to segue into the murderous part of the story when a pair of warm arms wraps themselves around me from behind and I turn my head just as Jasper lands a kiss to my lips.

Jasper Wilder is tall, dark, and handsome in the truest sense, with his dark hair, silver eyes, and a body put together just the way God intended. And I wholeheartedly approve of all of the above.

He tweaks his brows my way. ***How fast can we get out of here? I'm having a sudden craving for a bite of something sweet—like you.***

My cheeks heat as I chew on my lower lip. I'll be the first to say Jasper and I have been enjoying married life very, very much.

"Soon," I whisper.

"I'll hold you to it. What did I miss?" He dots a quick kiss to my cheek as well.

"What I'm hoping we'll miss altogether," I say as I quickly fill the three of them in on the dark conversations and thoughts I was privy to.

Jasper groans hard. "Murder, huh?" he says, pulling out his phone. "It's not happening on my watch."

Leo shakes his head. "Mine either."

"I'm calling in for extra foot patrol." Jasper excuses himself for a moment as he barks out orders over the phone.

"Bizzy, would you mind taking over my donut duties?" Leo hands me the platter of sweet treats. "I'm going to do a quick loop up and down the street." He takes off before I can say a word.

Sherlock nuzzles his head against my leg. ***More donuts for us, Bizzy.***

"Amen to that," I say, popping another one into my mouth.

Jasper heads this way once again. "Where's Leo?" He cranes his head above the crowd.

Emmie nods toward the gazebo. "He went that way. He's just taking a quick look around."

"I'd better join him." He lands a soft kiss to my temple. "Whatever you do, stay out of trouble."

"Trouble?" I practically gag on the word, but it's too late. Jasper is already threading through the crowd. "The way he said it you'd think I deliberately went looking for it."

Emmie cocks a brow. "Face it, Bizzy, you're not exactly a rabbit foot these days."

Fish lets out a quick yelp that actually sounds more like a laugh. ***Jasper is right. Steer clear of trouble, Bizzy. You're amassing quite the killer reputation.***

I make a face, but before I can translate to Emmie, something over at Suds and Illuminations catches my eye. It's Macy looking as if she's having a rather heated discussion with her blonde not-so-friendly counterpart.

Emmie and I speed over, and Macy is quick to take the platter from my hands.

Ember scoffs at my spicy sister. "I'll wring your neck if you try to sabotage all that I've worked so hard for."

"*You* worked so hard for?" Macy squawks. "You just opened your doors! But don't you worry your fake little head about it. Your doors won't stay open for long. This town is loyal to me. You and your shop are going down." ***I'll see to it myself with a little help from my friend the baseball bat. My brother-in-law is a cop. He practically owes me a gimme. He'll look the other way if he knows what side his Bizzy Baker toast is buttered on.***

I shoot a look to my sister. Jasper does not *owe* her a gimme.

"Is that a threat?" Ember balks. "If anything happens to this place, I am going to haunt you until you die. And you will regret the day we met."

"I'm one step ahead of you because I already regret the day we met!"

Ember's chest bucks with a silent laugh. "My business is going to succeed even if it kills me to do it."

"Your business is going to tank even if I have to kill *you* to do it."

Ember's mouth rounds out. "Get out of here. You don't belong on this side of the street."

"Oh, I do belong on this side of the street. I belong on every side of the street in this town because it happens to be *my* town," she snips at her old friend before offering the crowd before her a contrived smile. "I'm offering up scrumptious sweet treats on behalf of the Founders' Day Festival. In fact, I think I'll offer them up to some of your patrons as well—while I tell them all about the deals they can get across the street." She speeds into the establishment with that tray of donuts, and Ember snarls in her wake.

"Please excuse my sister," I tell her, but she's quick to wave me off.

"I'm not worried about it. I've dealt with far more spirited personalities." She glances to the brunette to her left, the same one that internally called her a brat not more than ten minutes ago. "Bizzy, meet Marigold Sweet, my stepmother. She can attest to my innocent intentions when it comes to opening up my dream shop. Marigold loves my father almost as much as I do." She winks her way. "Of course, my father loves me more. I'm his only child. And blood is thicker than water." She cackles, giving the brunette a playful swat on the arm.

The woman stretches a tight smile. "Ember is driven, all right. Nobody will deny her that." She winks my way. "Nice to meet you, Bizzy. If you'll excuse me, I think those donuts are calling my name." She heads into the store just as Emmie attempts to hold out the tray in her hands.

"I've got some right here!" she calls out, but it's too late. "They're apple cider donuts," she says, waving the tray toward Ember. "I baked them fresh this morning."

Ember lets out a hearty moan. "Donuts are my weakness. I'm Ember Sweet," she says to Emmie. "Welcome to Suds and Illuminations, the very place for all of your soap and candle needs." She quickly snaps up a handful of sweet treats and immediately begins to nosh on them. "So good!" She moans once again before something to her left snags her attention. "Flint!" she calls out as a dark-haired man with a clean-shaven face and dimples comes up. He looks to be in his early thirties, handsome to a fault, and just as brooding while dressed in a well-fitted suit. No sooner does he land by our side than he sheds what looks to be a well-rehearsed smile.

"Ladies." He holds out his hand. "Flint Butler, newly elected council member. Thank you for your votes if indeed I had them."

"Congratulations," Emmie and I say in unison. We often respond at the very same time in the very same manner, mostly because Emmie and I are basically the same person sans a supernatural quirk or two.

Ember clears her throat. "Now now, ladies, he's all mine." She bubbles with a laugh.

"That I am." His smile pulls a notch tighter. ***And if I have my way, that not-so-good time ends today.***

My mouth falls open at the thought.

A crowd moves in, and the two of them drift off to greet the masses as I pull Em off to the side and fill her in on his dark thought.

Emmie tweaks her brows. "It sounds like the identity thief is about to have her perky bubble popped. That's too bad. I don't wish a broken heart on anyone."

"Me either." I glance back and note Flint in what looks to be a heated argument with another man, about the same age, lighter hair, this one is wearing a flannel and jeans. The man he's with holds out his hand and Flint gives it an angry slap, but it didn't quite look like a high-five or a handshake. "Look at that."

Emmie leans in. "You think we should call Leo and Jasper?"

No sooner does she say it than the two men part ways. The man in the flannel glares over at Ember before turning and stalking off in the opposite direction.

Emmie sighs. "Why do I get the feeling Ember Sweet isn't so sweet after all? She does seem to like my donuts, though," she says as we watch her snap up a few more from the tray my sister is holding in front of her.

"That might be the only sweet thing about her."

Emmie drifts off to make sure the refreshment tables are still fully stocked with plenty of donuts for the entire state of Maine while I walk up and down the street, taking in the jovial crowd and keeping an eye out for anything nefarious, but there doesn't seem to be anything but joy in Cider Cove today.

The high school orchestra begins in on a cheery tune while Mayor Woods belts something out over the speaker regarding the town's centennial. But I tune her out as I crane my neck for signs of my sister or her feisty old friend turned nemesis, but there's no trace of either of them.

I scoop Fish into my arms and dot a kiss to her furry little forehead. "I'd better head over to Suds and Illuminations and make sure Macy isn't making good on that homicide she threatened."

Sherlock barks. *I hear something, Bizzy. I think I hear cats.* He strides ahead with a violent jolt, and I'm hardly able to hold onto the leash as he leads the way.

Cats? Really? Fish groans. *Oh for goodness' sake, Bizzy. Drop the leash. He knows his way home, and we're not lucky enough to lose him.*

"Fish." A small laugh strums from me as I playfully scold her. Fish and Sherlock get along well enough, but they tend to fight like siblings—or dare I say, cats and dogs. Deep down, I know she loves him. I'm pretty sure at least.

Sherlock threads through the crowd and leads us through a split between the buildings that houses Suds and Illuminations and the coffee shop next door.

A FRIGHTENING FANGS-GIVING

"Sherlock, where are you taking us? This leads to the alley."

Cats! Cats! He barks and sniffs his way along as he continues his charge.

Alley cats, bleh. Fish sticks her tongue out, and I can't help but laugh.

"You started off as an alley cat, remember?" It's true. I found Fish behind Macy's shop when she was just a few weeks old, and we've been as close as sisters ever since.

Sherlock stops abruptly and gives a soft bark as he comes upon a small box that seems to be moving.

I lean in and gasp as I spot not one but *three* black and white striped kittens with stunning blue eyes.

"Well, aren't you adorable!" I'm about to bend over and pick one up when I spot a boot lying to the side of the box. I step around the box, and to my horror, that boot is still very much attached to a body.

"Oh God." I kneel down and check the woman's pulse.

My sister won't have to worry about Ember Sweet ripping off her style or her shop anymore.

Ember Sweet is dead.

3

Two things happen simultaneously. One, I scream my head off. I don't care how many dead bodies I stumble upon, I will never get used to it. And two, I text Jasper.

I glance back to poor Ember lying there, and I force my head to turn away. And when I do, I spot a half-finished cigarette lying near the back door to Ember's shop. It's one of those ultra-skinny cigarettes called Sassy Slims. I remember them because they used to market them heavily to women. All of the ads had polished looking businesswomen walking briskly with a Sassy Slims dangling from their fingertips.

My mother used to smoke for a while when I was growing up, and I recognize that pink ring around the filter. In fact, I can still smell the faint scent of menthol lingering in the air, and it brings back memories of my mother when she'd walk through the door after enjoying one of those death sticks, as Hux used to call them. We were all thrilled when she quit.

I study the cigarette for a moment longer. It's only half-finished, and it makes me wonder if it was finished in haste.

No sooner do I hit *send* on that text than both Jasper and Leo materialize before me, along with a rather healthy size crowd.

Bodies ooze out of the rear of Suds and Illuminations, the same door I'm guessing Ember Sweet stepped out of just before she landed on the ground, and every single person gasps in response to seeing the poor thing lying here helpless.

Georgie howls, "Oh my goodness, Bizzy!" She waves me over to the box full of kittens that I had momentarily forgotten about.

They're mine! Sherlock barks. **I found them! I get to keep them! A box of kittens! And they're all mine, all mine!**

Fish growls, **That's nonsense, and you know it, fleabag. You can't just say they're yours. Haven't you learned anything from Jasper and Bizzy? If you want to keep them, you have to lick them.**

My lips invert. Jasper and I have said more than once *I licked you, you're mine*. Gross, I know, but we think it's cute.

Fish yowls as she cranes her neck to get a better look at them, **My, oh my, aren't they adorable? My goodness,** *they look just like me! I bet we're related somehow. Oh, Bizzy, we have to keep them. Tell Georgie to keep her mitts to herself.*

"Let's see," I say, heading over and quickly scooping up all three squirming cuties.

Help!

Get me down!

Why are these people screaming?

"Oh, they're terrified," I say as I look to Georgie. "I don't know who these belong to, but they were the first things I saw when I came back here. Sherlock sniffed them out. Would you watch them for me? I'll take them off your hands as soon as we get back to the inn."

"Are you kidding?" Georgie takes them from me, and I help her land them back in the tiny brown box they were sitting in to begin with. "Just try to pry these from my cold dead hands. Finders keepers, Bizzy! And I've got me some kittens!" Georgie shouts with the glee of a madwoman as she takes off toward Main Street, and I cringe because I'm pretty sure shouting for glee at a murder scene is highly frowned upon.

The brunette I met earlier, Ember's stepmother, Marigold, intercepts Georgie and picks up one of the kittens, nuzzling it against her cheek for a moment before saying something to Georgie and setting it back in the box. I can tell she's naturally nurturing. Even in this dark moment she wants to make sure those kittens are safe.

Macy pops up next to me, her eyes agog as she stares out at Ember.

"What the heck happened? Did she pass out?" She sucks in a quick breath as she looks my way. "You offed her for me, didn't you?"

"What?" I smack my sister on the arm. "Do not say that out loud ever again. There are people here, all of which have ears—the better to hear the murderous rumors you're starting."

"My goodness," Macy pants as her horror quickly morphs into something I'm not proud to say looks a lot like delight. "Ember Sweet is dead?" ***Wow. I either have a very good sister who cares far too much about that crappy shop I run or I'm able to kill people with my mind. To think, I was wishing a tree would fall on the girl less than an hour ago.*** "A tree didn't fall on her, did it?"

I avert my eyes. "I have no idea what happened to her."

Leo barks for the crowd to move back just as a swarm of sheriff's deputies arrive on the scene.

Jasper comes over and drapes his arm around me. "What happened, Bizzy?"

"Sherlock—he was leading me this way and he found a box of kittens. That's when I saw Ember. I checked her pulse. I thought maybe she passed out, but she was gone. And then I texted you."

He blows out a breath. "Her mouth has remnants of powdered sugar, and she has a donut in her hand—one of Emmie's."

Macy gasps. "Emmie's the killer?"

"Would you hush?" I hold my finger to my lips as I give a quick look around. "Emmie did not kill that poor woman." A horrible thought hits me. "Oh no, Jasper, you don't think she had an allergic reaction to one of the ingredients, do you?"

"At this point, everything is a possibility. The coroner will determine the cause of death, and I'll make sure you're one of the first to know since that donut puts the café on the hook."

"Thank you." I shudder as I look back over at the scene. The tall, dark-haired woman, Marigold, looks visibly shaken. Her eyes are swollen and red, and her back shudders as she spills silent tears.

Jasper follows my gaze. "I'd better head back, Bizzy. Stay safe. Accident or not, I don't want you getting tangled up in it either way."

He takes off and Macy leans in. "I can't believe this is happening."

"Me either."

The blonde we met earlier comes out of the shop and shrieks once she spots Ember.

"Oh my God! *Why*?" She begins in on a horrible chant of that single word, *why,* and the crowd quiets down to a hush. Her attention snags our way, and her grief turns to rage in an instant. "You!" She stalks over to Macy. "You said you were going to get even all because of this stupid rivalry the two of you had!"

Macy stiffens. "What? Really? *Hardly!* I opened my shop first! It's clear Ember was determined to rip me off in any and every way in an effort to make me miserable!"

The crowd gasps.

Fish belts out a sharp mewl, **Run for cover, Sherlock! They're going to stone her. Or in the least throw donuts at her.**

Sherlock whines, **I'll do my best to protect her. Why couldn't they throw bacon? I'm much better with bacon, but donuts are a close second.**

"Macy," I hiss. "This isn't the place."

The blonde woman steps in close. It's the same one Ember introduced as her business partner, Willow Taylor.

"You killed her! You said I hope you choke on those donuts and now she's dead!" Her voice hikes to surreal octaves, and yet the band plays on down at the other end of

Main Street. "You are a killer, Macy Baker! And I'm going to make sure justice is served just as cold as your murderous heart. You're not getting away with this." She stomps off back into the shop as a stunned silence fills the air.

Macy growls, "What are you looking at?" she roars at the crowd before they quickly look away and the alleyway explodes in hushed whispers.

"Macy." I close my eyes. "Why don't you get back to Lather and Light? Close the shop for the day and go home. I'll call you when the dust settles."

"I'm not going home with my tail between my legs, Bizzy. It's the kickoff for the Founders' Day Festival. It's already shaping up to be the busiest day of the year, and a very good start to the holiday shopping season. I'm a Baker. We don't throw in the towel—especially not for Ember Sweet. I'm sorry she's gone, but I sure as heck don't have to go with her. I'll talk to you later." She scowls over at the body. *Farwell, my old friend. It didn't have to end this way between us. And yet I'm not entirely sorry it did.* She shudders at the dark thought that just flew through her mind. *I wish it didn't.*

She takes off and I hold Fish tightly.

Tell me she didn't do it, Bizzy, Fish mewls as she taps my chest.

I shake my head. "She didn't." I hope.

Sherlock navigates us through the crowd as I try to inch my way closer to the mouth of that back door that leads to Suds and Illuminations. And soon enough, we come upon Marigold once again, sobbing silently to herself.

"I'm so sorry for your loss," I say as the woman looks my way.

Her eyes are filled with crimson tracks, and they look backlit from the tears brimming in them.

She shakes her head. "Thank you. I can't believe this is real. I just spoke with her father. He's a mess."

"Can I help you get home? Is he on his way here?"

"No, that's okay." She lifts her fingers, dismissing the idea. "He's on safari in Africa. Big game hunting. He'll be back soon enough. I have my car down the street. I'll be able to drive myself home." She sniffs hard as she looks over at Ember. "She had a good life." ***It could have been better if she wasn't so damn difficult.*** She lets out a heavy sigh. "I'm sorry. I'd better go. Ember lost her mother as a child, and I'm her only family here. I suppose I'll have to start thinking about arrangements and whatnot."

"If it helps, I manage the inn at the end of the street. If you need help with anything, I'd be glad to offer up my services."

"Oh, thank you." She blinks back. "I might take you up on that. Warner most likely won't be back for days, if that. And

Lord knows it was bad enough being in that drafty mansion with just Ember. I don't want to be there alone. I might check in for a few days if you have a vacancy."

"I certainly do. I'll have a room for you as soon as you can get to the inn."

"Thank you, Bizzy. I'll go throw a few things into a bag. Let me just make a few more calls." She steps away a few feet, and I spot Jasper and Leo pointing to something on Ember's sweater as they begin to photograph it.

"Jasper?" I call out, and he looks my way. I shrug over at him as if to ask what they're looking at without the use of words.

A fingernail with brown glittery polish, he says. ***A press-on or something. It's not Ember's.*** He lifts his brows my way. ***It's not yours, is it?***

I shake my head as I hold up my bare fingernails his way for him to inspect.

But I happen to know exactly who has brown glittery nails—my sister. Here's hoping all of her acrylics are still intact.

Sherlock barks and I look down.

"Hey, big guy." I offer him a quick pat on the back. "I know this is hard. Let's get out of here," I whisper.

Look, Bizzy*.* He barks again. ***To the left, toward that big tree.***

I glance that way, and sure enough, I see two men who look as if they're having a heated exchange. It's Ember's boyfriend, the councilman, Flint Butler, and that same man with the dirty blond hair he was arguing with earlier. It looks a little less volatile than it was before but twice as heated.

Huh. Flint looks far more angry than he does upset over the fact the woman he loves is lying dead in an alley. The two men look equally frustrated, but neither of them is grieving. But then again, people show their grief in different ways. And it's still so new, I'm sure they're both in shock.

Willow steps out again and muscles her way to the front of the crowd as she gets as close as she can to Ember's body without crossing the caution tape Leo just set up. I can't help but note that from the back she looks just like Ember, just like Macy.

I inch my way toward her.

"Willow?" I cringe a little as she turns around because I'd hate to see that heated exchange she just had with my sister spill my way. "If there's anything I can do to help you, please let me know. I'm the manager at the inn. Just ask for Bizzy."

"The business is so new." She shakes her head. "Ember was doing everything." ***Partially because she was a bossy control freak.*** "I'm not sure what to do. If I close the doors, I'll have nothing." ***But I do have something right now, and that's relief. I never thought I'd say this,***

but a part of me is exhilarated at the thought of having my life back. Ember is gone. It's as if a nightmare has come to a conclusion, and I can breathe freely again. She pushes out a deep breath. "Thank you, Bizzy. I'm not really all that business-minded, so I'm guessing I'll have my hands full."

"It'll come to you, I'm sure."

"We'll see."

Leo creates a bigger barrier, forcing us to step away from one another, and the crowd moves between us.

She's dead, a voice says with perfect calm as it comes to me clearly. ***And now all of my troubles are gone forever. Goodnight, Ember. Sleep tight. I'm sorry I had to do it, but you left me no choice.***

I crane my neck. The voice seems to be coming from across the way, but I can't tell if it was a man or a woman.

My feet carry me in that direction, and I stop cold once I spot four familiar faces staring down at Ember. Flint, the blond man, Marigold, and Willow stand almost shoulder to shoulder as the crowd presses in against them.

And I have a feeling one of them is the killer.

4

The Country Cottage Inn is perfectly enchanting any time of the year, but fall makes this overgrown mansion with its ivy covered-walls look every bit as cozy on the outside than it does on the inside.

The entry to the inn has been festooned with a garland of silk fall leaves, and a pair of twin wreaths made out of maple leaves hangs on each of the stately doors that lead inside. To the right of the entry there's a large cornucopia with squash and pumpkins spilling from it, and next to that there's a life-size turkey carved out of wood with an adorable expression on its cartoon face. Pumpkins and amber mums fill the pots out front, and there's a scarecrow staked next to the three-tiered fountain that sits to the left.

There's a blue cobblestone path that leads to and around the inn, all the way to the right where the Country Cottage Café is located in the rear of the building. The café has an expansive patio that overlooks the majestic Atlantic as well as the sandy beach that lines the cove. To the left of the inn and dotting the acreage around it sit more than thirty cottages that are available for lease or as nightly rentals. Jasper and I happen to live in one, and Emmie and Georgie live on the grounds as well.

And way off to the left-hand side, the inn has its very own pet daycare center called Critter Corner. The inn is listed as one of the most pet-friendly resorts in all of Maine, and that's a title we wear proudly.

The interior of the inn is cavernous with its gray wooden floors and dark wooden paneling along the walls. There's a grand staircase that sweeps up to the second floor where the guest rooms are, and just about every one of those is booked straight through January. The holidays are the busiest time of the year for the inn since so many people choose to stay here while they visit with relatives. And as much as I love the holidays, a part of me can't wait to ring in the new year.

Fish sleeps at her usual post, right up front on the marble reception counter, while Sherlock is curled in a ball by my feet. Usually, he's up front and center, taking his duties as the official welcoming committee very seriously, but he's so enamored with the sweet kittens he hasn't left their side once.

And seeing that Nessa, one of my employees, and I are holding the little cutie pies, he hasn't taken his eyes off of us either.

"I'm in love with them," Nessa coos. Nessa is a dark-haired beauty who happens to be related to Emmie. She's also a recent college grad who views her time at the inn as nothing more than a stepping-stone, but believe me, I'm thrilled she isn't stepping away any time soon. "I wish I could take them all, but I have Peanut, and the only cat he cares for is Fish." Last year Nessa adopted Peanut, a tiny black and white pug mix that is as cute as his name suggests.

Grady glances our way.

Grady Pennington is an Irish looker who also just so happens to be a recent college grad who keeps threatening to fly the coop.

"I can't take them either," he says. "But I'm sure if you put up a sign that reads *free cats*, they'll be gone in a hot minute. Maybe throw in a batch of these donuts to go along with them," he says as he pops another apple cider mini wonder into his mouth. Emmie dropped off a huge platter of them at the counter for the guests fifteen minutes ago, and there are only a few left.

Grady lifts a brow my way. *But knowing Bizzy, she'll let them hang out for a month at least before she gives them away. I'm starting to think animals are the key to her cracking all of those homicide cases. I'm not sure why, but I'm positive I'm right.*

He is, but I won't confirm it. The animals always seem to help crack the case, they're just that intuitive.

"I'm not just giving them to the first person who wants them," I say as I hold the one in my arms close. "There needs to be a vetting process."

Nessa belts out a laugh. "In other words, you want to keep them all to yourself."

Grady nods my way. "Just a heads-up. When I got here this morning, the guest log kept moving to a different location." He points to an opened notebook that typically sits on the counter, allowing the guests to leave their thoughts and suggestions. "Every few minutes I'd find it somewhere else, the back counter, under the counter, the grand room. I even found it in the café when I went to grab some donuts. And there wasn't anyone else around but me. You don't think any of those ghosts are still lingering from that haunted doll display Georgie forced upon us last month, do you?"

"I promise you, it's not a ghost." No sooner do I say the words than the lights begin to flicker.

Nessa lets out a rather *ghostly* moan. "I don't want anything to do with the dead, Bizzy. Can't you hire someone to walk through this place while burning sage or something equally as kooky to clear the place of any lingering spooks?"

"No," I tell her. "Because the inn isn't haunted. And I don't want to accidentally set it on fire."

A thick crowd bustles on in, along with an icy breeze, and Nessa hands the two kittens in her arms my way as both she and Grady get right to work.

I spot Georgie in the foyer, gripping the handle of something white and boxy, so I head on over to see if I can help. Her gray hair is wild and free, and her crimson and orange tie-dyed kaftan looks festive and seasonal.

I'm about to say something when I note an entire herd of women holding the same boxy plastic contraptions, along with overstuffed duffle bags, as they make their way toward the ballroom.

"What's going on?" I ask, almost certain I'm going to be sorry.

"Your mama and I have opened up the monthly crafts session to the quilting guild. We thought it'd be fun to put some stitches together. Don't worry, Biz. I've got Jordy in there working out the situation with the electrical."

Jordy is the handyman here at the inn, and I trust his judgment when it comes to just about anything. He's Emmie's brother, and my ex-husband. The marriage lasted less than a day. It involved Vegas, hard liquor, and an Elvis impersonator—need I say more?

Georgie grunts as she shifts her sewing machine to her other hand. "These mean machines aren't going to run themselves, they need to be juiced up. Speaking of which, I ran into Emmie outside, and she's bringing over some hot apple cider, coffee, and donuts. You should join us. It's BYOSM." She leans over and dots a kiss to each of the cuties in my arms before tossing Sherlock a bit of bacon from her pocket. She's been known to keep a strip or two on her person in the event a pork fat emergency arises. And one always seems to pop up.

Sherlock barks. **Hands off the kittens, Georgie. I won't trade them, not even for bacon. He sniffs the salted meat. But we can't just leave this lying on the floor either.** And just like that, he promptly licks it up.

"Do I want to know what BYOSM means?" Truthfully, the answer is no, but since I'm the keeper of this insane asylum, it's sort of my duty.

"Bring your own sewing machine, Toots! Juni ran out this morning to pick one up for herself. They're pricey, but they're worth the fun—except for when you accidentally sew your fingers together. That's not so much fun." She holds up a bandaged hand as she rushes past me.

"Ouch," I say just as my mother rushes past me.

"I'm late for class," she says, wheeling a large bright red suitcase behind her that I'm guessing has a sewing machine tucked inside it. She does a double take before backtracking my way.

Mom is in great shape for her age. I'm not sure where she's sent her wrinkles, but she doesn't have many of those to show for her age either. Her dark blonde hair is shoulder-length and feathered circa nineteen eighty something, and she holds strong to the same sense of style she had back then, too. She's a preppy to the max, with her cable knit sweaters and popped collars. She used to run her own real estate empire after she and my father split, but she's since retired—and apparently taken up quilting.

"Oh my stars," she coos as soon as she spots the furry trio of cuteness I'm holding. "Where in the world did these angels come from?"

"I have no idea." Okay, so I have some idea. Last night I let them know I could hear their thoughts and understand them. They mentioned something about being delivered to the alley by a nice man who said he was sure they would find a nice home quickly. I didn't dare tell them that the seemingly nice man had dumped them in the back of an alley. Maybe he was hoping someone from one of the local shops would find them? And, well, that's sort of what ended up happening.

She moans as she takes them in. "Aw, they look just like Mistletoe and Holly." Mom adopted a pair of kittens last Christmas, and I've never seen her so attentive to any living being before. Now that her kids are grown and gone, those cats really filled a void I don't think either of us knew she had. "But I'm afraid I can't take on any more. What are you going to do with them?"

"God only knows," I say.

She lifts a finger. "Come into the ballroom and we'll figure this out. Oh, and I want to know all about your latest murder!" she trills as she speeds that way. "Your sister told me about the body you found. You really have a knack for that!" She gives a thumbs-up as she falls in line with the thicket of other women drifting in the same direction.

"Good grief." I cringe. My mother can make anything I do sound like a budding accomplishment newsworthy to brag to her friends about. But let's face it, I haven't exactly given her much else to brag about.

I'm about to head that way when my brother strides in looking rather miffed, and by his side is an equally sour-faced Mackenzie Woods. Although, her cranky disposition is much more perennial than his is—or at least it used to be. Now that Hux and Mackenzie are the real deal, it wouldn't surprise me if I saw a steady decline in his jovial state.

Mackenzie Woods can make a grown man cry. I'm just hoping that grown man doesn't turn out to be my brother.

Mackenzie laughs at the sight of me. Her hair is spun into a tight bun, and she's donned a cranberry power suit, her go-to wardrobe essential.

"Well, if it isn't the little killer who could," she muses. "You really are trying to outdo yourself, aren't you? I can hardly wait to see what carnage you have planned for Cider Cove this Christmas. A double homicide, perhaps?" She bubbles with laughter, but neither Hux nor I join in. *Here's hoping Georgie and that ex-convict of a daughter are involved on the receiving end of that one.*

"Not funny," I say. "What's going on?" I take a moment to scowl at the two of them. Neither of them has any business at the inn.

Mack gives the cute little kittens in my arms the stink eye. "What's with the sewer rats? Don't answer that." She gives each one a gentle scratch over the ears and bites the air as if threatening to eat them. "I'm here because Hux promised me waffles out by the sea." She sniffs. "And don't forget, the Founders' Day concert at the cove is in a week. We're counting on the inn to provide refreshments and maybe some more of those donuts you used to kill your latest victim—the town will be hoofing the bill. Try not to kill any members of Sugar Shack. They happen to be my favorite band." She gives Hux a kiss on the cheek. *Let's hope Bizzy doesn't slaughter one of us in our sleep. It'll most likely be me.* "I'll go order those waffles." She takes off in haste, clip-clopping her way toward the café, and Sherlock gives a quick bark in her wake.

She's never given me bacon, Bizzy. Not once.

Huxley offers Sherlock a quick pat on the back. "Macy's heading over and we're going to talk about this mess she's gotten herself into. You do realize the best friend of the woman who died is accusing Macy of doing the deadly deed. Someone wrote the word *killer* over her shop window this morning."

"Oh no, that's terrible."

"That, my sister, is defamation," he corrects. "Macy wants to sue Willow Taylor, the surviving partner of that shop that opened up across the way for slander."

A groan evicts from me. "I wouldn't do that."

"Well, I would." Macy crops up, looking bright-eyed and bushy-tailed, and ready for revenge on whoever thought it was a good idea to deface her storefront. Her blonde hair looks almost snow white in the light, and she's donned a denim jacket with matching blue jeans. "I won't be called a killer when I didn't harm a hair on that ridiculous woman's head." *I wanted to, but that's beside the point.*

"Macy." I wince as I give a quick look around. "You can't call her a ridiculous woman. Don't speak ill of the dead. It will only make you look bad."

Huxley nods. "Or like the killer."

The three cute little kittens in my arms begin to mewl at once.

She's a killer!

Oh, we're all dead.

Sherlock, help us! We're too young to die!

"Now look what you've done," I say. "You've scared the kittens."

Huxley chuckles. "Don't feel bad, little ones"—he pats them on the head—"Macy Baker has the capability to scare grown men."

Emmie whips by with a giant platter of fresh apple cider mini donuts, and the three of us helplessly head in that direction as the sugary scent casts its spell on us.

Inside, the ballroom is light and bright. The floor is heavily carpeted with a leaf motif. There are over two dozen round tables set out, with a mountain of fabric over them, and a sewing machine dots them all like a mechanical centerpiece.

We load up on donuts before heading to where Georgie and Mom have their goods laid out.

"What do you think?" Georgie holds her arms out. "We're calling it the Crazy Quilt Lady Club."

Mom rolls her eyes. "*You're* calling it that. The rest of us are calling it the Cider Cove Quilting Guild. Apparently, they've been meeting for years in an old renovated barn. Come to find out, they like the ballroom much better."

Georgie waves her off. "They're just jealous because my wonky quilts are selling like hotcakes." She pulls one off the table with its black and orange patches that make it look perfect for fall.

The trio of kittens in my arms cranes their heads that way and mewls with approval.

Georgie sighs as she drapes it around her shoulders. "I just can't figure out how to make them into a jacket. It turns out, there are far too many moving parts to that pattern. I stayed up all night trying to solve the riddle of the wonky jacket sphinx. And I learned long ago there are only two things worth losing any sleep over. Number one, a man in your bed."

I jut my head forward. "What's number two?"

Georgie nods. "*A man in your bed.*"

Mom laughs. "You're wrong on both counts." She holds the quilt up with her hands. "And I don't know about turning this into a jacket. That's going to be tough." Mom pinches the corners of the quilt and holds it out to inspect it. "But given time, I think it would be a very good idea. You're really onto something with all this whip stitching and fringed fabric. These take half the time to construct as your run-of-the-mill *pieced* quilt. I can see the appeal."

Juni whizzes past us with an oversized box that has a picture of a sewing machine on its side and she lands it onto Georgie's table.

"Mama!" she cries out as she staggers over to where her mother proudly displays a quilt over her back. "That's it! Who cares about a quilted jacket? Women all over Maine will be tripping over themselves to get ahold of a Georgie Conner's wonky cape!"

"*A wonky cape!*" Georgie howls, and the two of them break out into an odd little jig.

Mom sighs. "They'll be tripping over themselves, all right. If I were you, Bizzy, I wouldn't sell those deathtraps at the inn. Think of the liability." She taps her temple before heading back to the piles of holiday-themed fabric folded neatly at her station.

A pair of warm hands encircles me from behind as Jasper drops a kiss to my cheek.

"Good morning." He nods to Huxley and Macy. He's already said good morning to me in a far more delicious way, and a naughty smile twitches on my lips just thinking about it.

Hey, beautiful. He dots a kiss to my cheek. **You haven't forgotten who I am, have you? Because if you're murky, I can take you back to the cottage and refresh your memory.**

A laugh bucks through me as I give him a wink. "Who are you again?"

"Bizzy." Macy clasps her hands together as she looks my way. "Thank God you're sleeping with the lead homicide detective. Jasper, I demand you set everyone in this twisted town straight. And while you're at it, make that brat, Willow Taylor, come over to my shop and wash the lipstick off my window."

Jasper's chest widens. "I'm sorry, Macy. I'm afraid I can't do that. In fact, I think I need to see your hands."

I may have filled Jasper in on Macy's acrylic nails last night, and suddenly I'm regretting the decision.

"What for?" Macy holds her hands out, and sure enough, one of the acrylic fingernails on her right hand is missing. "Are you looking for traces of red lipstick? Because if you think I've desecrated my own shop, you're insane. Bizzy, I command you to end this matrimonial farce. Clearly Jasper is a plant sent to destroy our family."

Jasper gives a somber nod. "Macy, we found an acrylic nail that matches yours at the scene of the crime—embedded in Ember Sweet's sweater. Care to explain?"

Hux mutters a few salty words under his breath. "She's not saying anything." He rolls his head back. "I'm officially acting as my sister's attorney."

A FRIGHTENING FANGS-GIVING

And I'm officially—unofficially going to do whatever I can to make sure my sister doesn't fry for this.

5

"*No*," Jasper says without wavering as the morning light slices through the curtain.

We've been rolling around in bed for the better half of an hour, mostly to get the day off to the right start, but I may regrettably have brought up the possibility of seeing Willow Taylor today.

"*Yes*," I tell him as he pulls me close and he lands another mouthwatering kiss over my lips. "No, fair. I specifically remember you saying you'd never deny me anything," I tease while drawing a line down his chest with my finger.

A dull laugh pumps through him. "Is it too late for me to rephrase that? Because I thought it was a given I wouldn't want you hanging around with killers."

"Unless you know something that I don't, Willow Taylor is still just a suspect. Besides, Macy already said she was going to talk to her today. And we both know once Macy puts her mind to something, she's unstoppable."

He groans and I take him in, with the dark stubble on his cheeks, his hair slightly mussed, his eyes as pale as lightning.

Jasper lets out a heavy sigh. "I think we both know she's not the only unstoppable Baker sister." He frowns my way. "Okay. I concede. But just this once—and only because you're headed to her shop. I'm going to allow both Macy and Main Street to give me the false sense of security I need to get through the day. Do me a favor and text me when it's over."

"Will do." I shrug up at him. "We still have an hour before either of us has to walk out the door."

He lifts a brow. "I've got a few ideas on how to kill the time."

I land my finger over his lips. "Show, don't tell."

And Jasper gives me a demonstration for the ages.

Suds and Illuminations is closed until further notice. I should have figured. But Macy was in such a rage, she spent all day tracking down Willow Taylor, until she finally succeeded. It turns out, Willow Taylor likes to spend her time at a bar called the Happy Hour located in the underbelly of a rather seedy town to the west of us called Edison.

Once Georgie and Juni got wind of the fact Macy and I were headed to schmooze with a suspect at a place called the Happy Hour, they quickly materialized in the backseat of my sister's car.

Jasper is working late, and seeing that I do need to eat, not to mention mind the three of these women lest they burn down all of Maine, I'm front and center for all the action. I've donned my best fall boots, my peacoat, and here we are staring up at the behemoth establishment wondering what kind of an adventure waits for us inside.

Fish mewls from the tote bag cinched onto my shoulder, *I smell food, Bizzy. We're lucky we didn't bring Sherlock. He's not nearly as obedient as I am around human food.* She nuzzles her face against my chest. *You do know how much I like fresh fish. It's in my name, for Pete's sake. If you don't mind, pick up a bite for me, would you? I've never eaten out at a fancy restaurant before.*

I wasn't going to bring Fish along for the ride, but Georgie scooped up the kittens and put them in a little front carrier papoose I had lying around. I have several, but this one has a small platform for them to stand on, and the front is made of mesh so they can see everything around them.

Georgie has it strapped to her chest, and the kittens have been giggling and snipping at one another all the way over. And now the three of them are crying out Fish's name like a choir.

The bar itself is tucked inside an oversized long cabin of a building with a sign out front that reads *Welcome to Happy Hour, where every hour is happy!*

Juni grunts, "You got your booze, you got your happy tappies." She pats her stomach. I think she meant tapas, but I'm not up for correcting her. "I may never leave."

Juni has donned her traditional biker gear, a dark leather jacket, matching short leather skirt, fishnets, and flashy red heels. There are only two trains of thoughts when it comes to her accouterments: either people love it—a category almost exclusively reserved for newly released convicts—or they think her cognition is a little mixed up and she's trying to emulate a hooker.

Georgie nods. "And look"—she points to a small sign in the window—"happy hour includes a Thanksgiving dinner plate sampler. Ooh, I love me some Thanksgiving. Let's get on inside, girls. There's food, booze, and boys to be had."

Georgie is causing a bit of a scene herself with the way she's chosen to dress. She's got on her requisite kaftan, in a rich shade of mustard, and over that she's tossed one of her wonky quilts, an orange and yellow wonder with prints of a cartoon turkey stamped over it, and she's cinched it around her neck with a giant pumpkin-shaped brooch. The wonky cape is alive and well, and right here in Edison with us.

Honestly, I've sported that same look a time or two late at night when trekking from the sofa to the fridge while on the hunt for a midnight snack, but I'm not sure I'm brave enough to parade around town in it.

Macy growls over at Georgie, "Which superhero are you supposed to be? Captain Crazy? Or just plain Crazy Cat Lady?" She jabs a finger at the trio of kittens and sends them into a frenzy. Her short platinum bob has had a fresh cut this afternoon and looks just as razor sharp and dangerous as my sister's tongue. She's donned a brown leather jacket with matching boots that ride up well past her knees, and she's finished the look with large gold hoop earrings that are big enough to work as bracelets.

The kittens mewl in turn.

Oh, she hates us.

I think she's going to eat us.

Perhaps she's a witch looking for a familiar? Is that food I smell?

I do my best to stifle a laugh and Macy lands her wild eyes on mine.

"You're one to laugh. Why in the heck is Fish here? Haven't you ever heard the words, *no shirt, no shoes, no sanity, no service?*"

I make a face. "I know, but as soon as Georgie grabbed the kittens, Fish insisted on coming. She's protective over them."

And equally as hungry as they are, Fish purrs with a touch too much excitement.

"Besides"—I say to my ornery sister—"you mentioned we were going to make this quick, remember? I want to be home before Jasper gets to the cottage. And didn't you say something about having a hot date?"

Macy grunts at her own reflection while sprucing up her hair with her fingers.

"That's right, I do have a hot date." She sniffs. "But it doesn't mean I'm going to let a hottie go to waste if I find one inside. Lucky for me, I don't have a limit on how many men I can date in a single night."

"Me either, sister." Juni rocks her hip to Macy's. "I say we leave the crazy cat ladies in the dust and get down to it."

The two of them speed inside while Georgie and I get congested in the entry as we try to walk in at the very same time. The cats yowl, Georgie yelps, and I groan because Macy is right—I am clearly entering without my sanity.

Inside, it's dimly lit, the scent of fresh roasted turkey permeates the air, and the sound of a sappy country song filters through the speakers.

We follow Macy through a thick crowd of mostly inebriated and very happy to be here patrons as we make our way to one of the tall tables near the bar that is apparently for standing only seeing there's not a chair in sight. A few people are dancing near the front and the sound of intermittent laughter threatens to pierce my eardrums, but once I get a glimpse of the buffet, all sins are forgiven.

"Oh wow! It really is like Thanksgiving," I say as my stomach begins to growl on cue.

Georgie brushes her shoulder to mine, and I can't help but notice she's getting some odd looks from the tables around us.

"Speaking of Turkey Day, what's the lowdown on who we're going to spend it with? You've got two families now. That means we get two dinners, right? Right?"

Georgie has spent every Thanksgiving with me for as long as I can remember, and there's no way I'm abandoning her now.

"Dad and Gwen hopped on another cruise," I tell her.

My father and Jasper's mother have been a thing for over a year now. It's sort of weird, I know.

Georgie shakes her head. "And here I didn't think they'd last."

Macy grunts, "Clearly they're just staying together to spite all the naysayers. Me being one of them."

"Me being another," I say. They spent last month cruising, and no sooner did they disembark than they hopped right on another seaside voyage. "Jasper's brothers and sister haven't mentioned anything about Thanksgiving. I think I'll invite them all to the inn. Since Cider Cove is having their first official Thanksgiving Day parade, the café has been swamped with orders for full Thanksgiving dinners to go. I'd better stay close to make sure things run smoothly—that way I can give Grady and Nessa the afternoon off."

Macy nods my way. "If you've got the turkey and pie, I've got the time. But I plan on dining and ditching. There's nothing better than snuggling up with my laptop after stuffing myself like a turkey and shopping until I drop. Ooh, and I'll need a pumpkin pie to go. It's my tackling fuel when it comes to scoping out all the best deals."

Juni shakes her head. "I'll be there with jingle bells on. There's nothing like a Thanksgiving Day meal to put me in a three-day coma. In fact, I'm going to start right now." She smacks my sister on the arm. "Dibs on the beefcake at the buffet with the tats and the red bandana." She takes off, and the three of us look in that direction to see a barrel-chested man with a beer belly lapping his pants. The bandana in question is wrapped around his arm, I think he's stuffing dinner rolls into it, and the tattoos look worn out and disfigured by time.

Macy sighs. "Juniper Moonbeam is going to make some optometrist a very rich man."

"No fair." Georgie snarls. "Juni always gets the cream of the crop. Don't worry, kittens. We'll get our mittens on some beefcake yet." She leans our way. "They're my secret weapon. I took them out on the town today, and I may as well have been wrapped in bacon the way the men drooled at the goods."

"Georgie." Macy's cheeks flicker. "I know for a fact you went to the Cider Cove Senior Center. Those men were drooling for another reason entirely. But just to be safe, I'll take a kitten after I finish my dinner. I'm willing to test your bacon-wrapped theory."

Fish touches her paw to my chest. **We should give them names, Bizzy. Something just as cute as they are—like say, Fish One, Two, and Three?**

I squelch a laugh. "I think Fish wants us to name the kittens, Georgie."

"Oh, they've got names." She holds open her quilt as if she was about to flash us. "Meet Pumpkin, Spice, and Cookie. I don't know who's who, but they do and that's all that matters."

The three of them mewl in unison.

I'm Cookie.

I'm *Cookie*, another one bleats.

You can both be Cookie, the third pipes up. ***I rather like Pumpkin Spice.***

I touch my finger over the one with a white patch over her forehead. "You can be Cookie." I give the one with a peach nose a quick pat. "And you are obviously Pumpkin." I look to the kitten with the most stripes. "And you, my sweet girl, are Spice."

Georgie scoots past me. "I'm taking my cool cats and loading up at the buffet. Try not to arrest anyone until I get back. But don't wait up for me either. I'm gunning for a slice of beefcake myself. There's no reason Juni should get to have all the fun."

She takes off just as Macy grips me by the arms.

"There she is," she hisses while pointing behind me.

Sure enough, Willow Taylor is laughing with an orange fruity concoction in her hand while talking to two men at once and I gasp at the sight of her.

"Wow, Macy. Not only does she look just like you, but with that brown leather jacket and thigh-high boots, she's a dead ringer."

"The operative word being *dead*." Macy glowers at the woman, and Willow does a double take in our direction before heading on over without hesitation.

"Here she comes," I grit the words out like a ventriloquist. "Play nice. On second thought, don't play at all. Let me handle this."

Willow lands her elbows to the table and doesn't bother to hide the disgruntled look on her face.

"What are the two of you doing here? You didn't follow me, did you?" *And here I thought* **Ember** *was far too interested in my business.*

"Follow you?" Macy hisses. "So what if I did?"

"Wrong answer." I moan as Fish ducks her head into my tote bag.

Willow scoffs. "Look, I don't want any trouble from you. Your beef was with Ember, and she's cold in the morgue." *And it feels like my birthday and Christmas rolled into one.*

I blink back at the horrible thought.

Her birthday and Christmas? Who says something like that?

"Yeah?" Macy's eyes grow wide with rage. "Well, maybe she's cold in the morgue because *you* put her there. And now you're trying to pin it on *me*."

Willow laughs at the thought. "You're almost as nuts as she was."

Nuts? The woman clearly did not care for Ember. So why go into business with her?

"*I'm* nuts?" Macy's voice hikes up over the chipper song bleating through the speakers.

"Hold your horses!" Georgie hobbles back with two heaping plates of what looks to be a full Thanksgiving dinner. And my God, does that turkey ever look juicy. The mashed potatoes have a nice well of brown gravy pressed into them, and the stuffing looks light and fluffy with bits of sausage in it. I'd eat all the above with my hands tied behind my back if I had to.

Georgie passes me a spare fork as if reading my mind.

"As you were, ladies." She nods to the dueling blondes in front of us. "Keep the jabs above the waist, no face shots, nothing below the belt. Winner gets the hottie with the tie cinched around his forehead doing the sprinkler move out on the dance floor. Now let's get ready to *rumble*!"

Macy leans dangerously close to the blonde in front of her.

"You think *I'm* nuts? I'm not the one running around trying to be me. I *am* me. And don't think you're fooling anyone with that blonde mop on your head. I can see your red roots from here!"

"I can see your *dark* roots from here, but I couldn't care less." She runs her fingers through her tresses. "Besides, I'm done with this hairstyle. I've already made an appointment to have it dyed back to my natural color. I loved being a redhead. I never wanted to change it."

"I get it." Georgie shakes her head as she swallows down her next bite. "You did it for a man on a dare in bed. It happened to me once. Only I ended up shaving myself bald. I had red hair, and I loved every feisty minute of it."

"You did?" I marvel over at her, choosing to ignore the story of the man who once graced, or disgraced, her bed.

"Yup." Georgie waves a cornbread muffin at us. "And I was as fiery as they came. But don't worry about going silver. The flame just gets hotter, the men get spicier, and the dares require a safety harness."

Willow offers a friendly laugh. "Good to know. And I changed my color a few weeks ago. It was Ember's idea." She glances to the ceiling as if the thought annoyed her. "But she's not here anymore, so back it goes." **Ember may have been obsessed with stealing this girl's identity, but I'm not interested in being anyone but myself. I should buy a box kit and dye it red myself. Every time I look in the mirror, I see Ember.** She shudders at the thought.

Macy squints as she leans in. "Admit it. Ember was nothing but a copycat who wanted to *be* me. Her obsession knew no bounds, and that cheater-brand shop she opened up was nothing but a means to aggravate me."

"You're not wrong." She swills her drink and takes a sip. "And by the way, I saw what it said on your store window this morning. I didn't write it. I don't care whether or not you believe me either. I just want to be done with all of this." *And as soon as I ditch that soapy mess I've landed myself in, I'm going to forget about this entire town.*

Fish pokes her head out once again. *Did she just admit that Ember was out to get Macy?*

I give her a scratch and nod.

"Willow?" I lean her way. "Why was Ember so obsessed with Macy? Did my sister do something to her?"

Macy clears her throat, her blue eyes dart around the establishment, and I'd know a guilty look on my sister's face if ever there were one. I try to pry into her mind, but nary a thought runs wild.

Figures.

Willow shrugs. "Only you know, Macy. But I can say with one hundred percent conviction that you did something to really set her off. Ember is a pistol under normal circumstances, but whatever you did launched her into full destruction mode—and it was your destruction she was gunning for. So come on, spill it. What did you do?"

Macy breaks off a piece of Georgie's cornbread and pops it into her mouth.

"Can't talk," she mumbles through a mouthful. "Trying to eat."

Well, that says it all.

"Willow, you were at the shop before Ember—you know..." I say. "What do you think happened?"

She flits her eyes back to my sister. "I saw the two of you going at it. Ember kept shoveling those donuts into her mouth, and the next thing I knew she was dead."

Georgie spikes her fork in the air. "The donuts were dusted with poison!"

The crowd around us quiets to a hush for a moment before resuming their intermittent laughter. I'm pretty sure once they got an eyeful of Georgie in her cape, they dismissed the poison donut theory.

I bet she's right, though.

Willow gasps as she wags a finger in Macy's direction. "You brought over that platter with the donuts on it! Oh my God, I had one." Her hand flies to her neck. "I should get tested. I bet I have toxins coursing through my veins as we speak. I could be on the brink of death myself."

Georgie moans through a bite. "You're still looking good, kid. Don't worry. We redheads are hot as firecrackers right to the very end. If you do end up toes to the sky, you're gonna be a beautiful corpse."

"Good to know." She tips her drink toward Georgie.

"Wait a minute," Georgie grunts. "You don't think the killer is out to get you, too, do you?"

"I don't know." Willow lifts a brow in my sister's direction. "Are you?"

Macy belts out a laugh. "I may have gotten my death wish, but I didn't dust those donuts with anything fit to land her underground."

"*Macy*," I scold as Fish belts out a meow at the very same time.

Oh, she's guilty, Bizzy, Fish mewls. **We both know it. The only thing to do now is find someone else to pin it on. If all else fails, there's always Juni. She rather liked the security guards during her last incarceration.**

I nod because she might be onto something.

Willow tips her head as she examines my sister. "How would you like to buy a boatload of soap and candles?"

Macy's lips part. "Are you selling your inventory?"

"Darn right I am. I'm still on the hook for the lease for the next eleven months, but if I stop using the funds allocated to inventory, I might have enough to pay at least six of those."

Macy groans. "I hate to break it to you, but we share the same landlord. You're on the hook for the next eleven or they'll ruin you financially in an effort to get what's theirs."

Georgie raises her hand and nearly gags on the food in her mouth.

"I'll take it!" she squawks. "I'll take over the lease. I'll open a wonky quilt shop, and I can sell my mosaics there, too. I've been waiting for an opportunity to fall into my lap and here it is. And it would figure a sassy redhead and a dubious murderer would open the door to my good fortune. Well-played, universe. Well-played." She glances down at the trio of cuteness. "Hear that, kids? We're getting the band back together and going into business!"

"Georgie." I shake my head. "We should probably run some numbers before you commit to anything." And I'm not exactly sure who that band consists of either.

She frowns my way. "I'm crunching numbers as we speak, sister, and I like what they're saying." She looks to Willow while hitching her thumb my way. "We'll talk when the killjoy is nowhere in sight. Word to the wise: keep your dreams to yourself around this one or she'll take the hammer of her opinion and shatter them to pieces."

"*Pfft*," Macy huffs. "Try growing up with her."

"Try living with her." Georgie sighs. "And I'm not even in the same cottage. I'm sorry, Bizzy, but I predict Jasper will be giving you the heave-ho by Christmas. The man can only take so much."

"*Georgie.*" A laugh gets caught in my throat, but I refuse to give it because it's so not funny.

Fish yowls, **Ignore them, Bizzy. We've got a suspect at hand.**

Who's the killer? one of the kittens mewls, and I'd like to know the answer to that myself.

Willow shudders. "Anyway, I stepped into Suds and Illuminations this morning and everything in that shop was turned upside down."

"What?" I all but spin her my way. "What do you think happened? Do you think someone broke in?"

She shakes her head. "Oh no. It was definitely Ember. She came back. As in her *ghost* was the one responsible for the destruction."

Georgie slaps her hand down over the table. "And I bet she flew over to your storefront Macy and wrote the word *killer* in red lipstick onto your window! It all makes sense now. Case closed." She comes shy of winking at Macy. "You've got a ghost on your hands, Toots. I'd sleep with one eye open if I were you. And maybe bathe in holy water. Better yet, find a cute priest and bring him to bed with you just as a precaution. You throw a ghost into the mix and things are bound to get freaky. What I wouldn't pay to see that."

Willow nods. "I'm convinced Ember wrote those words, too, Macy. She really had it in for you. Haunting you from the great beyond isn't a total shocker. Ember was determined in this life. I can only imagine what she's capable of in the next."

"This is terrifying," I mutter to myself. And it has nothing to do with a supposed ghost. Mostly it has to do with the fact Macy might just take Georgie up on her blasphemous advice.

"Willow, who did you last see Ember with?" I try my hardest to steer this conversation back to solid ground.

Good direction, Fish meows. ***It's not as if she was about to admit to doing the murderous deed herself.***

"*Myself*, but I didn't kill her." Willow rolls her eyes. "Believe me, I wanted to. Ember and I were like sisters. We fought like cats and dogs." ***Mostly rabid dogs ready to take one another down.***

Fish mewls again, ***That's a fantasy propagated by a silly euphemism. Sherlock and I get along whenever we want to. Mostly I don't want to, but he insists.***

"You fought?" I shrug, trying to come off casual and not hungry to shake her down for answers. "About what?"

"The usual—clothes, men." ***That witch had such a stranglehold over my life that I don't even recognize myself when I look in the mirror. I like Macy Baker, for Pete's sake. When Ember was bent on destroying someone, she knew exactly which buttons to push. And that's exactly why she pushed mine. And how I***

hated her. Macy hated her, too. "You know what, Macy? I'm going to buy you a drink. Actually, I'm feeling generous. I'll buy you all a round." She whistles as a waitress heads this way, and soon we've all put in orders for the same fruity concoction Willow is holding.

Georgie points over at me. "Make Ms. Priss' a virgin. She's got a stuffy and uptight reputation to uphold." She leans toward Macy. "Let's hope her husband doesn't have a stiffy."

Macy shrugs. "He'll be a pro at cold showers by New Year's."

I take a moment to scowl at them both before forcing a smile at the waitress.

"I'm sensitive to alcohol." I nod as she takes off with a wink. It's true. Liquor might be quicker, but for someone endowed with telesensual powers, it's the quickest way to lose my mind—by way of reading a thousand others all at once. "Willow was anyone angry with Ember? Outside of Macy, of course." I shoot a look to my sister.

Macy certainly knows how to make herself look guilty.

"Who was angry with her? Lots of people." Willow takes a breath. ***Me for one. I was furious, but that's thankfully in the past now.*** "Let's see, Marigold and Ember were pretty close, but you could sense some tension there. Obviously Hunter. He was about to blow a hole through the roof just a few days before we opened."

"Who's Hunter?" I ask, trying to place the name with a face, but I'm coming up empty. "I thought her boyfriend's name was Flint?"

"It is." She nods. "Hunter was her ex. They dated on and off for a few years, and things sort of came to an end about six months ago. He was a lawyer, but I don't think he does that anymore. Or was he a stockbroker?" She taps her chin with her finger. "Whatever he was, he was very, very angry. I thought he was going to kill her last summer the way those two were ranting at one another. And then there's Flint. He's the one with the cheesy politician smile. His career is finally kicking off. But if you ask me, I think he was about to kick Ember to the curb. Toward the end, something didn't feel right whenever the two of them were in the same room."

Macy clears her throat as she checks her phone. "Would you look at the time? I've got a date in less than fifteen minutes." She taps away at the screen. "I'm going to ask him to pick me up right here. I'd better get to the restroom and spruce myself up." She riffles through her purse quickly before glancing our way. "Any of you ladies have a razor I can borrow? I seem to be all out."

"A razor?" I gape at my sister as I try to wrap my mind around why she feels the need for shaving speed—here of all places.

Both Willow and Georgie do a quick check of their bags. Willow comes up with a toothbrush, and Georgie is the first to slide a bubblegum pink razor across the table as if it was a trophy.

"Oh, thank God." She cinches her purse to her shoulder. "Willow, we'll get together and talk about that inventory. You do have top-of-the-line products, but seeing they have the patina of death on them, I'll be expecting a deep discount." She looks to Georgie and me. "And I'll see you girls tomorrow." She takes off, and a thought hits me.

"Macy, you drove!" I call out after her, but it's too late. She's gone. I turn back to Willow. "All right," I snip without meaning to. "Willow, I know you're hiding something. What was going on with you and Ember? You might be putting up a front, but I can tell you're furious with her. I'm good at reading faces."

"Yeah," Georgie spouts off. "And she's even better at reading minds."

Willow chuckles as I widen my eyes at Georgie.

"You're right, Bizzy. I wasn't thrilled with her. I poured all of my life savings into opening up a store I wasn't even interested in. I had to borrow from my grandmother." ***Worse yet, I had to lie and tell her I was headed to nursing school with the money. It's what I've always wanted. It was my dream, but Ember wasn't having it.***

I blink back. Something isn't right. How could Ember make her give up her dream?

"Willow, if Macy doesn't buy all of your inventory, I'll take what she doesn't for the spa at the inn. In fact, why don't you come down anytime you want. You can have a full treatment on me."

"Really?" She presses a hand to her chest. "Expect to see me sooner than later." She knocks back the rest of her drink. "Great seeing you ladies." She points over at Georgie. "You and those crooked blankets are going to go far."

"*Wonky quilts*!" she shouts up over the music as Willow disappears into the crowd.

My stomach growls like a bear, and I'm about to head to the buffet just as a tall, dark, and dangerously sexy homicide detective steps before me.

"Bizzy Baker Wilder." Jasper does his best to frown, but there's a smile rising on the corners of his lips. "How did I know I'd find you here?"

I cringe a little. "Because you figured out exactly where Willow Taylor spends her free time?"

He nods. "And I had a sneaking suspicion you'd be spending yours here as well." He glances down at the tote bag wiggling by my side. "Is that Fish?"

Georgie honks out a laugh. "Have cat will travel. Get a load of these, Wilder." She unzips the top of the mesh compartment she has the kittens locked up in, and one right after the other jumps out, into her food before landing on the floor and darting away into the crowd.

"Oh my God! The kittens!" I shout in horror. And no sooner do the three of us go in three different directions to look for them than the entire place breaks out into screams of horror and we hear the words *mice, snakes,* and *werewolves* all at the very same time.

Juni pops up with that tattooed farmer of hers, and the two of them all but knock the buffet over as they struggle to catch one of the kittens trapped beneath it.

Bodies jump and hustle to the door while those little kittens dart across the floor from one end of the room to the other like little white streaks of lightning.

Finally Juni manages to wrangle one, but not before sinking her entire hand into a vat of mashed potatoes—honest to God, there was no good reason for her to do so. I'm guessing she was squeezing some food-based fantasy in there somewhere to take advantage of the moment.

Jasper chases a kitten down at the bar and causes about ten different drinks to sail to the floor in the process.

Georgie takes off her quilt and waves it around as if she was a matador, in hopes to catch the final little rascal. But it's not the kitten who ends up running through Georgie's quilt of wonky terror—it's me on all fours.

However, all is not lost. I spot a striped cutie under one of the tables, and both Fish and I trap her between us.

I reach over and snatch her up, much to the crowd's delight, and soon the Happy Hour is back to its pre-hysteria madness.

All three kittens get placed back where they came from. And Georgie swears on her cornbread stuffing she'll never let them out again, which only sends them into a panic.

Jasper and I enjoy a Thanksgiving dinner, and despite the fact he's not all that thrilled with me, Jasper Wilder is very much examining me with a gleam of devilish delight.

We round up Juni and Georgie and get back to the cottage where we go *round* after round with each other.

Jasper and I are good together. And I bet if we teamed up to find Ember Sweet's killer, we'd be unstoppable.

In fact, I'm going to propose we do just that.

Tomorrow, of course.

I'd hate to ruin the momentum.

6

"There are many ways to cook a turkey," Emmie says as she looks to both Jordy and me right here in the Country Cottage Café.

It's the morning after the Happy Hour fiasco, and I had both Emmie and her brother in stitches trying to describe how mortifying it was playing the part of the bull last night. Both Emmie and Jordy are used to me humiliating myself in grand fashion, so to picture me on all fours wasn't all that shocking.

The kittens wriggle in my arms. I've got all three of the little cuties in a fur-lined basket, and for the most part they seem thrilled to be out and about. Fish and Sherlock are in the ballroom—correction, *crafts* room—manning the infantry of women, the flying fabric, and the sewing machines, which are busily whirring. Not to mention Georgie has a never-ending supply of bacon for Sherlock, and my mother is babying Fish. The rest of the guild is in love with them both and are busy drowning them with attention. It's a win-win for everyone.

Jordy nods. "I'll be manning the turkey fry, right outside the back of the kitchen."

Emmie takes one of the kittens from me. "We're frying them in peanut oil."

HELP! The tiny tot in her hand squeals and Emmie laughs.

"Not you, little one." She's quick to comfort the feisty fuzzball, aptly named Spice.

Jordy takes another bite out of his pumpkin waffles and gives a hard moan. Emmie has brilliantly revamped the menu for fall, and the guests have been enjoying pumpkin spice everything. The savory fare is just as seasonal with its rich stews, chilis, and, of course, chowder.

And seeing that I have zero survival skills in the kitchen, both Jasper and I are thrilled to have a functioning restaurant less than five minutes' worth of walking distance. Living at the inn is like living at a resort—a resort who's very existence rides solely on my shoulders. But I try not to think about that.

"I ordered a smoker, too." He looks to his sister.

"Ooh, that's right." Emmie snaps her fingers. "We're offering smoked turkeys as well. You wouldn't believe the orders we're getting this year, Bizzy. And once they taste how juicy our turkeys will be, expect to have the orders double for Christmas. I've got a new recipe for the roasted turkeys as well. All you do to lock in the juices is give them an aggressive salt rub under the skin. That stops the meat from drying out once they're cooking. But before I slip them in the oven, I stuff pats of butter and tons of honey under the skin as well. It adds just enough sweet and savory to every bite and we don't have to brine them."

"You're making me hungry for turkey," I say, snatching up another apple spice mini donut, and Emmie frowns at the platter for a moment.

"I can't believe someone used my sweet treats as a means to poison someone. If I find that killer, I might just *kill* them."

"Easy, girl." Jordy bumps his elbow to hers before looking my way. "Did Jasper ever find out what substance they used?"

"Nope. But I'm guessing that's the next bit of news we receive."

Jordy glances behind me. "I have a feeling we're about to receive it right now."

Jasper appears at our table with his hair slicked back and still dewy from the shower. He's donned a dark wool jacket with a matching scarf, and both just so happen to set off his pale gray eyes.

"Hey, hot stuff." I give a little wink. "Take a load off and eat some donuts with us. What are you doing back in Cider Cove so soon? Don't tell me they fired you," I tease. "But if they did, we could always start our own detective agency. Rumor has it, we make a great team."

"We do." He dots a kiss to my cheek before landing in the seat next to me. "But getting fired might have been a better start to my workday." He sheds a pained smile. "You didn't poison the donuts, did you?" he asks as he takes up a handful.

"I leave that fun to my sister," I say, snatching another one up myself.

Jordy nods to Jasper. "So what did they use? Weed killer?"

"Close." Jasper tips his head to the side. "Strychnine. A white powder that could blend seamlessly with the powdered sugar these donuts are dusted with."

Emmie clutches at her neck. "That's terrible. But strychnine? Couldn't she taste something like that?"

"She could," Jasper points out. "But if she was gobbling them down like everyone seemed to be, then it might have been too late. It's extremely toxic and death could occur in minutes."

Jordy shakes his head. "So where does one get their hands on this stuff?"

"It's a rodenticide. Able to be purchased only through pest control professionals. Used mostly in bait for gophers and rats."

Jordy's lips part. "I have access to them. I use bait like that all the time. I set them under the lawn in various places."

I look to Jasper. "That means anyone can dig them up and repurpose them."

Jasper's chest expands. "You're right. This is anybody's deadly game." His eyes pierce mine. "Did you find anything out about the mystery man Willow brought up last night?"

I told Jasper everything about my exchange with Willow Taylor.

"No," I say. "But only because I haven't begun to look." I drop a kiss to one of the kittens. "I've got too much furry cuteness keeping me occupied."

"Good." His brows pinch. "Because you're going to need a distraction. Forensics reported that Ember Sweet had human tissue cells under her fingernails and foreign blonde hair on her person." He sighs as he says it. "I'm on my way to Lather and Light. I need to ask your sister to come down to the station with me so we can run a few tests."

Emmie, Jordy, and I all groan in unison.

"No way," Jordy say. "Macy isn't the killer."

"Maybe not." I hold that basket of cuties close. "But she's sure starting to look guiltier by the second. She's essentially giving the killer a pass. The more attention is given to Macy, the less attention is given to whoever really did it."

Jasper's phone goes off. "I have to take this." He rises from his seat as he looks my way. "You want to come down to Main Street with me? I might need you to defuse the bomb."

"Sounds good. I'll text Huxley. No doubt he'll want to be there."

"Perfect. Tell him to meet us there in a half an hour. I think those pumpkin waffles are calling my name." He takes off for the patio to tend to his phone call.

"Excuse me, ladies," Jordy says as he lands his ball cap back on his head and rises. "I've got to check the electrical panels. The way those breakers were going off yesterday you'd think we really do have a ghost around here."

"We don't have a ghost," I whisper. "And I wouldn't say that out loud. Grady is convinced we have one rearranging our office supplies at the front desk." The words that Willow said last night about Ember haunting Macy come back to mind, and I shake the thought out of my head.

Jordy takes off, and I shudder just thinking about having something nefarious and otherworldly going on right here in Cider Cove.

"Don't worry, Bizzy." Emmie takes another kitten from me. "Macy will be proven innocent. *Feisty*, but innocent."

I nod. "And that feisty behavior is exactly why we're on the long road to clearing her name."

The kittens in her hands mewl.

"What are they saying, Bizzy?" Emmie squeals with excitement. Last month after Emmie found out that both Leo and I can read the human and the animal mind, she's been having lively conversations with both her dog, Cinnamon, and Leo's golden, Gatsby. Not that she wasn't before.

The one in her left arm looks up at her and yowls, *You don't smell like a killer. When will we find a home?*

The one in her other arm mewls, *A home without a killer, please.*

The furry cutie in my basket lets out a little yip. *I hope they serve Fancy Beast like Bizzy.*

I quickly translate, and both Emmie and I have a laugh over it.

"I'm going to find you all good homes," I tell them. "And I will make sure you are well supplied with Fancy Beast cat food. It's Fish's favorite, too."

Emmie moans. "I'd keep you all myself if I knew my dog wouldn't use you as chew toys."

"It wouldn't be a far cry from what Sherlock is doing to them at my place." I'm about to fill Emmie in on the adorable way the kittens nestle up against Sherlock's belly at night when I spot Marigold Sweet at the counter. I quickly excuse myself and head on over.

"Marigold?" I say as I come upon the polished looking brunette. Her hair is glossy and pin straight as it hangs below her neck, and she's wrapped in a peach trench coat as if she just came from a brisk walk in the autumn air. Her eyes glow like emeralds, and I wish mine would look half as entrancing. She really is a beautiful woman. "How are you liking the inn?" She checked in yesterday morning, but this is the first I'm seeing her.

"Oh, it's so great here." She gives each of the kittens in my arms a quick scratch on the forehead. "Just try to get rid of me. My husband isn't coming back for another two weeks. He says Ember would have wanted him to finish out his trip. He's right, but I could sure use him around." ***Not really. At least not yet. I need these feelings to die out. I'd hate for Warner to see me this way. I'm never jumpy, and if I've been anything since Ember bit the big one, it's been jumpy.***

I nod because that's completely understandable. Ember's death has *me* jumpy, and I wasn't nearly as close.

She glances to her phone. "I'll be taking care of the details, making arrangements, and whatnot. I'm afraid it will be nothing more than meetings with the morgue, with my husband's attorneys. Her father doesn't want a big to-do for her. We just want to get through this." She ticks her head over at the kittens. "These cats are so adorable." She coos, and they both mewl up at us.

Is she taking us home, Bizzy? one calls out.

Is she the killer? another cries.

Even though the kittens were in the alley at the time the killing occurred, they were emphatic that they could only see Ember.

"I spoke with Willow yesterday," I tell Marigold. "She says she's not reopening the shop. I guess they had a break-in."

"A break-in?"

I nod. "She said the store was trashed, products were everywhere. I think she's afraid whoever did it might come back."

"I bet it was Ember." Her fingers float to her lips. "She used to say the world couldn't get rid of her. If she had her way, she'd come back to haunt us all. And she has, Bizzy." Her chest pants wildly. "I woke up this morning to the sound of glass breaking. I was alone in my room and a vase that was sitting on the dresser knocked over. We didn't have an earthquake. And I was sound asleep up until that point. She's haunting me. I'm positive of it. And she's doing it to Willow, too. She hated all of us."

"Why did she hate you?"

Marigold's chest pumps with a dry laugh. *I could write a book, the list is so long. But I'm guessing this isn't the time for that.*

"She can't stand the fact that I married her father. She called me arm-candy for a solid year." She averts her eyes. "Ember was a spoiled little brat, and she never bothered to hide the fact. She cared more about her father's money than she did him."

"I take it he's a wealthy man."

"Generational wealth, mostly from oil." She nods. "It's a crime for one man to have so much money. But then, he's got Ember and me to spend it all. And believe me when I say, we were giving it all we've got."

We share a small laugh.

"What about Willow?" I shrug her way. "What do you think of her?" Maybe I could wrangle the truth from Marigold. I just know Willow was holding out on us last night about something.

She gives a quick glance over her shoulder. "Willow Taylor, if that is her real name, had some issues with her past. I don't know all the details, but Ember mentioned something once about owning her. She said when they met, Willow confessed to moving from Vermont because she was wanted on some petty theft charges. I guess her grandmother lives out this way. But she met up with Ember—and boy, did that poor girl pick the wrong person to unload her life on. Ember loved to have dirt on people. Manipulating their destinies was her favorite game. She already had all the money she could want." **Mostly**. "She wanted the power."

"Petty theft, huh?" I make a face. "I would think that would give Ember enough leverage to make her do anything she wanted. Including opening a candle shop with whatever funds she had." And not going to nursing school.

"That's right." Marigold blows out a breath as she looks toward the kitchen. "Ember Sweet wasn't so sweet after all. But it's no surprise to her father or me. She was just a product of the environment she was raised in. I used to think there was hope for her. But it's too late for that." **Maybe with time, she would have softened. But that's not a risk any of the people she was actively threatening were willing to take.**

My eyes widen. People wanted Ember Sweet dead. Lots of people. That means I need to interrogate those very people again and again until something begins to make sense.

A thought comes to me.

"Marigold, my sister feels really bad about everything." Or at least she should. "Especially because of the way she was acting that day. She wants to hold a candlelight vigil outside of her shop, and I told her I'd help get people to come. It's looking like it's going to take place next Friday." Because that date just so happens to work for me. Here's hoping I can get Macy to attend, let alone admit to people that she came up with the idea. Macy would no sooner hold a vigil for the girl than she would cook a turkey. But if she doesn't do her part to track down the killer, she'll be the one who's stuffed—right into a prison cell. "Willow said I should try to track down one of her exes. Hunter something?"

"Hunter Knox." She cringes. "Ember made quick work of him. Let's just say he's a prime example of what happened when you crossed her." Her body indulges in a mean shiver. "He used to be a well-respected pharmacist, but I think he's working at the docks now. I'm not exactly sure. I haven't seen him in a while." Marigold's order number is called, and she holds the ticket my way. "It's time to relax with some pumpkin spice pancakes. And I put in for a half dozen of those donuts on the side. Boy, are they delicious."

"They are. Enjoy."

"I will." She takes off to collect her tray. *I'll especially enjoy the donuts knowing that Ember Sweet got her just desserts with exactly this delicious treat. The irony of it all will never escape me.*

The irony won't escape me either.

Jasper orders up his waffles, and I sit with him as we discuss the case.

Ember Sweet wasn't so sweet after all.

A FRIGHTENING FANGS-GIVING

And unfortunately, that just opens the suspect pool right up.

Anybody could have done it, I suppose—with the exception of Macy, of course.

Let's just hope there's no more physical evidence linking her to the scene of the crime. Or she might just fry yet, and the killer will have plenty to be thankful for this holiday season.

7

The wind blows through Main Street like an icy poltergeist bent on vengeance as Jasper and I enter Lather and Light, my sister's soap and candle shop.

Instantly, the warm scent from a vanilla candle ignites my senses, and I have the sudden urge to curl up with a good book and read by the fire. Emmie offered to watch the kittens while Jasper and I came down to all but apprehend my cagey sister. And knowing Macy, I'll need both of my arms and my legs to do it.

The shop is painted a warm shade of coffee, and dotted along the entire store are old oak barrels brimming with my sister's merchandise. A few rustic looking tables line the middle of the store, leading all the way back to the register, and on each one is an artful display of soaps and candles in every shape and size. Everywhere you look fall décor is lining the shelves and walls. There are enough silk maple leaves in here to outfit every barren tree on Main Street. There's just something about the orange and red leaves that gives me that warm homey feeling.

A few pumpkins are set out throughout the shop, and there's an oversized cornucopia on the counter in front of the register with colorful purse-size bottles of hand sanitizer spilling out of it. But that lavender wisteria tree bejeweled in twinkle lights that sits in her bay window is the crowning jewel of this place. Macy has hung miniature pumpkin and turkey ornaments from its branches, and in a few weeks she'll decorate it for Christmas as well.

It's hard to believe the same woman who owns and runs this innocent establishment is a person of interest in an active homicide investigation. That is, unless you've met my sister. Then it's entirely believable.

Macy looks up from helping out a small group of customers and quickly excuses herself as she makes her way over. Her hair is loose and freshly washed, and her blue eyes are heavily outlined with dark kohl and it really makes them pop. She's donned her signature leather jacket, this time in a dark maroon, and she's got a pair of cute little booties on her feet to match.

"Well, look who the cat dragged in." Her hot pink lips stretch into a smile. "You don't really have a cat with you, right?" She eyes my purse because I've been known to haul a feline or two around with me.

"Not today," I sing, trying not to sound too suspicious.

She squints over at the two us. "Oh, I get it. You're here to up your game in the bedroom." She makes a face at Jasper. "She's stalling out on you already, huh?"

I scoff at the thought. "I'm not staling out."

Her chest bucks with a laugh. "If she's as fun in the sack as she is on the street, I feel sorry for you. Hot tip: my sister gravitates toward dessert-scented candles. And if you really want to get her in a good mood, I'd feed her something sweet to go along with it. Ooh"—her eyes grow wide—"like those poison donuts I supposedly fed to Ember?" She makes a face as she glances behind her. "You know, when I came in this morning, I found all the front displays toppled over." She nods my way as if I should know where this is headed. "I think she's after me."

"What?" I shake my head. "I don't think that was the work of a ghost. That was probably a break-in. Jasper"—I turn his way—"that's exactly what happened to the shop across the street. Maybe we've got a candle-loving burglar on our hands?"

His brows bounce with amusement. "I'll check on that as soon as I get back to my desk. Macy, I'm going to help you set up a security camera in your shop." He purses his lips. "But we're not here for candles this morning. I'm sorry, but I'm going to have to ask you to come down to Seaview with me. We need to take your fingerprints and a few samples of your hair and skin cells."

Her eyes sharpen over mine. "Well, well. It looks as if I'm about to spend the rest of the morning at the Seaview Day Spa. But I'll have to be home in time for dinner. I have a hot date tonight."

Jasper chuckles to himself. "You'll be back in plenty of time. But I wouldn't leave the state if I were you. If Ember has your DNA on her person, this is going to get serious quickly."

Macy takes a breath. ***Perfect. Not only have I set myself up to look like the killer, I'm probably going to fry for killing the witch. If only I had done the deed, it would have been worth it.*** A smile flickers on her lips. ***But I'll have the last laugh. I always do. And I'll have it with both Hunter and Flint.***

I groan at the thought that just blew through her mind.

"Excuse me, Jasper. I'd like to have a word alone with my sister." I pull her over toward the discounted Halloween merchandise, one of which is a tin haunted house no bigger than a foot high that holds about a half a dozen votive candles to make it look as if it's glowing from the inside. I've had my eye on it ever since last year, and now that it's practically free, it's coming home with me. "That hot date you have tonight"—my lips press tightly because I'm half-tempted to out the fact I just pried into her depraved mind—"who is it with? And don't lie to me. I can read you like a book." More than she'll ever know.

She sighs a moment. "Okay, fine. It's with one of Ember's exes."

I suck in a hard breath. "Hunter Knox?"

"You know him?" She looks momentarily thrown by the fact. "Of course, you do. You're Bizzy Baker Wilder, supersleuth extraordinaire. Boy, what you lack in the kitchen *or* the bedroom, you certainly make up for in the investigative field. And good thing, too, because you're running out of rooms."

"Would you leave me out of this? How could you date her ex? *Why* are you dating her ex? Don't you know you look guilty enough?"

"Calm down. I was talking to Hunter as early as last week." **Right after Ember threatened me for dating her current boyfriend.**

I close my eyes a moment.

"Macy Baker," I hiss as I swat her on the arm. "You were seeing Flint, too?" I couldn't help it. I can only hold back so much.

Her mouth rounds out. "You really can read me like a book. And so what? He's hot, and he kept coming around to meet his future constituents while campaigning for city council. You know I have a stud muffin radar that I can control no more than you can control being a killjoy. How was I supposed to know he was dating my nemesis? And by the time we had gone out a few times, it was too late. She found out and accused me of trying to steal her man. She told me to watch out because she was about to take a bite out of what was mine. That's back a few weeks ago when she still had long brown hair. Fast-forward to the other day and I wasn't just looking at a doppelgänger of my shop, I was looking at a mirror image of myself. Not as cute, of course. And those boots she had on? It just goes to show, money can't buy taste."

"Macy! The woman is dead. For goodness' sake, when you get down to the station, please refrain from highlighting her lack of style. At least now we know why you ticked her off royalty. From what I hear, she was a loose cannon—blackmailing her way to power with any and everyone. It's not a shocker she opened up that shop. You're just lucky Willow doesn't feel the same." That conversation I had with Willow earlier comes to mind. "What did Ember do to Hunter?"

Macy blinks back. "Darned if I know."

"Wait a minute. Does Hunter have dark blond hair?"

"Yeah, so?"

"I think he might be the guy that I saw the day of the murder. He was having a heated exchange with Flint."

She giggles to herself. "I bet they were fighting over me."

"Or Ember." I glance in the direction of the shop across the street. "Where's Hunter taking you tonight?"

"Out." **There's no way I'm telling her we're headed to the Founders' Day Jamboree down at the Montgomerys' pumpkin patch. She'll have to pry that info out of my cold, dead hands. The last thing I need is her poking around and ruining my hot date. I've got a bale of hay to roll around in, and my little sister isn't a part of that naughty equation.**

I nod as a smile flickers on my lips. "Let's get this business at the sheriff's department over with so you can get ready for that hot date of yours."

I have a few ducks to set in a row myself. It looks as if I'll be heading to the Founders' Day Jamboree this evening.

Macy, Jasper, and I all head down to Seaview in a caravan. Huxley meets up with us, and Jasper escorts us to the forensics facility in the building that sits just behind the sheriff's station.

We watch as Macy is fingerprinted, swabbed, and otherwise processed by the lab in what I'm hoping will prove her innocence. They pluck a few strands of hair from her head and send us on our way.

Outside, Huxley glowers at our sister. "Tell me right now if you did it." The words come sharply from him. "The worst thing you can do is lie to your attorney."

She glances to Jasper, and he quickly volunteers to step back into the building, citing the need to make a phone call.

"Macy." I shake my head at her. "You didn't do this. Right?"

She takes a breath as she glances to the row of evergreens across the street.

"I'm not the one who finished her off, but let's just say those lab results won't come back in my favor. We may have had a physical altercation shortly before she perished."

A hard groan comes from both Huxley and me.

Hux nods. "I'm sorry to break it to you, Mace, but physical evidence works great in the courtroom."

I close my eyes. "I'm guessing the verbal threats you doled out will work pretty well, too."

"I didn't do this." Her words come out pressured. "I can't go to prison. I'm too young. I'm too pretty. My God, I've wanted to be popular all my life but not in there."

"Why did you have to date her exes? One of which wasn't even an ex yet," I spit the words out as I tap her with my elbow. "You could have had any single man in all of Maine."

Hux stiffens. "You dated her *exes*?"

"I'm sorry to disappoint you," she snips back. "But that's the way the relationship cookie crumbled. And you know what? I'm not sorry about it either. I really wish I smoked, because right about now I could really use a cigarette." She stalks off toward the parking lot in a huff.

Hux nods. "And I could use a drink. Hell, I'm going to need a bottle."

"You and me both." I shudder as Jasper comes back out and wraps his arms around me.

"Don't worry, Bizzy." He drops a kiss to my cheek. "The real killer is out there, and we're going to find them. It's just a matter of time."

Hux shakes his head at him. "You and I both know the farther we get away from the day of the murder, the harder it will be to track down the killer. Macy is up a creek without a paddle."

"She's up a creek, all right," I say. "One of her own making."

And now it's up to me to get her back on dry land before she's found guilty in a court of law for a homicide she had nothing to do with.

A FRIGHTENING FANGS-GIVING

Whoever killed Ember Sweet had better watch out. Their days of freedom are numbered.

They may have killed Ember, but there's no way I'm going to let them mess with my sister.

8

"Wonky capes! Come and get your red-hot wonky capes!"

It takes a few good seconds for me to accept what my eyes and ears are experiencing. I've brought Fish, Sherlock Bones, and the trio of cuties to the Founders' Day Jamboree out at the Montgomerys' pumpkin patch.

I've got Sherlock on a leash, Fish strapped to my chest in a papoose, and the triplets in a cat stroller with a mesh enclosure to ensure another scene like the one at the Happy Hour doesn't replay itself.

It's early evening, and since Jasper is working late, I've ventured out to the Founders' Day Jamboree all by my lonesome. I was under strict orders from Macy not to breathe a word of it to Georgie or Juni in fear they'd turn her red-hot date with a potential killer into a circus. But I can see fate and

A FRIGHTENING FANGS-GIVING

Georgie's wonky quilts—or capes as it were—had different plans.

I weave my way through the crowd. The Montgomerys' pumpkin patch is spread over a vast acreage. Throngs of people have shown up to celebrate. There's a live band singing covers of popular country songs, and a huge banner is strewn across the entrance that reads *Cider Cove, 100 years strong!*

But the star of the show seems to be the happy orange globes that rule the roost here. Everywhere you look there are artful displays of pumpkins in every shape and color. There's a three-tiered fountain that stands twenty feet tall at least, and instead of water, every tier is brimming with pumpkins. There are scarecrows with happy jack-o'-lantern heads scattered about, and there's a giant hollowed-out pumpkin carved into a carriage with a small bench inside, allowing people to take their pictures in it. There are even huge glob-like pumpkins, the size of small cars, out on display.

There are dozens upon dozens of booths that range from wreath making to pumpkin and gourd painting, and every craft under the sun seems to be represented and for sale.

And then there is the food. We're talking turkey tacos, deep-fried turkey legs, turkey kabobs, turkey burgers on brioche buns, turkey corn dogs, and last but not least, pumpkin spice funnel cakes. And as if the heady scent of deep-fried everything wasn't enough, the hint of vanilla and sugar in the air is clawing at my stomach.

Sherlock barks and jumps. *I see Georgie! I smell bacon, Bizzy. I bet it's coming from her pocket.*

Fish yowls, *Pull it together, furball! Bizzy is here on serious business. We've got a killer to catch. And he happens to be dating our Aunt Macy.* Fish twitches her whiskers my way. *I think your sister is his next victim. But in the event it's too late for her, I say we start hitting the food.*

I make a face. "It's too late for my sister in many respects. But I think she can hold her own for a little while. Let's say hi to Georgie."

I manage to push the stroller over the hay-strewn dirt until we land at the booth Georgie seems to have procured for herself. And to my amazement, she has a nice size inventory of her wonky quilts on display, all of them in keeping with the theme of seasonal hues and patterns of fall leaves and pumpkins. On the display table next to her, there's a large turkey made of tumbleweeds, and in a basket in front of it sit tiny bags of candy corn tied off with a black and white checkered ribbon with a sign that reads *turkey toes, one dollar each!*

"Bizzy Baker!" Georgie runs out screaming with her arms held wide as a crowd of women step over to inspect her wares.

"Fancy meeting you here." She pulls me into a warm embrace before pulling a handful of bacon out of her pocket and making Sherlock the happiest dog alive.

Georgie has donned her signature kaftan in a cheery shade of yellow, but it's not clearly visible because she also happens to be wearing one of her wonky quilts strapped over her shoulder and cinched at the neck by way of an antique looking silver brooch.

"Well, who have we got here?" She quickly unzips the mesh netting over the stroller and plucks out all three kittens at once.

Fish groans. ***Goodness. Here we go. I hope you're wearing your running shoes.***

"Don't you dare let them go," I tell Georgie as I take one of the squirming kittens from her.

"Hey, Pumpkin. Hey, Cookie." Georgie plants a kiss to each of their furry heads as their bright blue eyes siren out at us.

The kitten in my hand mewls, ***I'm Cookie.***

"This is Cookie." I wrinkle my nose at Georgie.

"And I'm kooky." She gives the tiny peanut a bump with one of her sisters. "So what are you doing here? Let me guess, you're trolling for turkey on a stick. Well, you came to the right place, kid."

"Actually, Macy is here somewhere with a man I was looking to question. Leave it to my sister to date within the suspect pool." I leave out the part where she's actually dating *two* of the suspects at the very same time.

"A suspect!" She waves a kitten at someone past me. "Ree! Get your preppy hiney back where it belongs. Break's over, sister. I've got places to go and suspects to question."

Before I know it, my mother appears with her feathered hair and popped collar looking like a fashion plate in a plaid peacoat and tan suede boots.

She gives me a quick embrace and takes Cookie from me.

"All right, kiddo," she says to the tiny tot. "Are you ready to man the booth?" She looks to Georgie. "I knew you'd take off sooner than later." She nods my way. "Don't feel bad for me, I'm getting thirty percent of the profits."

Georgie grunts, "You'd get more if you stopped trying to push them off as couch covers. These are works of art meant to be displayed on the backs of beautiful women. In fact"—Georgie snaps her fingers, and before I know it, she's draped a quilt over my shoulders and clasped it to my neck with a brooch in the shape of a giant turkey—"you're going to be my walking wonky billboard."

"Lovely." I press out a short-lived smile.

Mom gets back to the booth and offers to keep the stroller there in the event she needs to house Cookie, but Georgie isn't giving up the two she's holding.

The striped cutie in Georgie's right hand mewls at me, ***Tell Georgie if we come upon the killer, I'd like to be tossed his way. I've been sharpening my claws all day for this.***

I nod. It's true. My furniture can attest to it.

I quickly translate and Georgie belts out a laugh. "Feed these kittens an extra helping of that fancy food you give them. It's on me tonight, kiddos." She nuzzles each one and they mewl with approval.

Sherlock barks and stops short. ***There's Macy up ahead.***

"I see her!" I bump my shoulder to Georgie's. "She's getting on the hayride. And she's with the guy I saw roughing up Ember's boyfriend. It's her ex, Hunter." My adrenaline begins to pump at the sight of him. His dark blond hair is shorn short and he's wearing a tan coat with a plaid scarf.

"Oh, they're taking off," Georgie howls as she races ahead and her cape sails behind her like a kite. "Stop, thief!" she calls out, and I immediately regret anything and everything that's about to happen.

Georgie tosses herself and the kittens into the path of the tractor pulling a flatbed loaded with guests—all looking to have a good time no doubt—and the entire apparatus comes to an abrupt halt, nearly tossing off a half a dozen people.

"Whoa!" The driver takes off his ball cap and waves it at her in an aggressive manner. "Are you nuts, lady?"

Georgie moans. "You picked a fine time to flirt with me, mister. Catch me on the flipside."

A kind gentleman helps hoist Georgie and me onboard—pets included—and before we know it, we're seated on either side of Macy and Ember's ex like a pair of psychotic bookends.

"Smooth." Macy nods as the tractor starts up again and the hayride moves along. "Hunter, this is my sister, Bizzy, and her menagerie. Ignore the homeless woman shivering under a blanket. She's a white witch who has the capability to steal your soul if you look directly into her eyes. Many a good people have suffered because of her. And try not to judge their attire too harshly. The white witch is trying to start up a crooked quilt coven."

"Wonky quilt coven," Georgie corrects. "And I'm more into starting a girl gang. I'll be the leader, of course. Macy, you can bring in the cute guys, and, Bizzy, you can stand guard at the door." She leans toward my sister. "We'll have fun on the inside while she plays the part of the lookout."

Macy nods. "That was my childhood in a nutshell."

Hunter bucks with a laugh. "Nice to meet you both." He gives Sherlock a quick pat on the head. "I used to have a dog just like you. Best friend I ever had." *I would still have him, too, if Ember didn't swear she was allergic to the poor guy. I still can't believe I chose her over the dog. I'd give anything to have him back. Her, not so much.*

"Nice to meet you," I say just as Fish pokes her head out at him.

It's the killer! Fish yowls. *And we're stuck on this contraption with him. Quick, toss the kittens at him so they can claw his eyes out before he slaughters us all. We haven't even tried the turkey, Bizzy. Don't let him ruin our night.*

He leans in and squints over at Fish. "My, what a cute baby you have there." He chuckles as he gives her a quick scratch between the ears, and I can't help but like him. He seems nice enough. He's handsome enough, too, with smooth skin and bright amber-colored eyes. Marigold mentioned he was a pharmacist. Maybe he's a good match for my sister after all? With the exception of that little killer detail. Leave it to Macy to winnow out the hottie with murderous intentions.

"Thank you," I tell him. "I think they're both keepers." A thought comes to me. "In fact"—I motion for Georgie to hand over the kittens, and soon I'm juggling them as well—"I stumbled upon these little cuties in the back alley of that new shop in town, Suds and Illuminations?"

His eyes grow wide. "Small world." He flicks his fingers as if asking if he could hold one, and I let him take the one in my left hand.

I'm in the arms of a killer! The tiny thing swats her paws at him full steam ahead. ***I'm going to die! I'm going to claw his eyes out, and then I'm going to run screaming, all the way home!*** Her entire body squirms and fidgets.

"Hey there, little one." Hunter pulls her in and strokes her until she's purring with her eyes closed.

So much for having an attack cat on my hands. But truthfully, I like this version better.

A sharp mewl comes from the kitten I'm still holding. ***I want some of that, too, Bizzy,*** she yelps as she struggles to make her way over.

"Traitor," I tease as I hand her to Hunter, and soon they're both fast asleep in his arms.

Georgie coos, "This one is a keeper, Macy. He's a cat whisperer. Men like that don't come around too often. I wouldn't let him go if I were you." She leans toward Hunter. "If you get sick of this one, you come looking for me, hot stuff. I've got a bottle cap collection in my bedroom, you wouldn't believe. You bring the boozy, I'll be your floozy."

"And on that note"—Macy smacks her hand over Georgie's knee—"Hunter, why don't you tell us where you were on the night Ember Sweet was murdered? I don't see why we don't just cut to the chase." She glares my way. "You've already murdered my date."

I sink a little in my seat, but before I can plow through my brain in hopes to figure out a way to rectify this, Georgie moans and groans.

"Way to ruin the investigation." Georgie gives my sister a rather aggressive elbow check and nearly knocks her right off of this hostile hayride.

And now it's me moaning and groaning. Right about now, I'd like to send the both of them flying into the nearest pasture.

Sherlock whimpers, **I'm sorry, Bizzy. Maybe Georgie can give him some bacon? Bacon always makes me forget about anything else going on around me.**

He's not wrong.

Hunter's brows knit together as he looks my way.

"You must be talking about the investigation involving that murder. I knew the deceased. We dated for a time." **Worst year of my life.**

"I'm sorry for your loss." I offer a mournful smile, but mostly I'm mourning the last few minutes. "Macy tells me that Ember wasn't all that easy to get along with."

He gives a wistful shake of the head. "I would tend to agree with that." ***And that's the understatement of the year.*** "She certainly had a way about her. I'm not sure it was entirely her fault. Ember was given whatever she wanted from the moment she came into this world. Of course, losing her mother at an early age only made her father throw more cash and prizes her way. She was raised by an army of nannies."

"That sounds like a very lavish yet sheltered life."

Macy huffs, "There's a reason I called her the bubble-wrapped princess."

I make wild eyes at my loose-lipped sister. Obviously, Hunter had feelings for Ember once. I'm sure he doesn't want to hear people disparaging her now that she's gone.

Hunter's chest bounces with a dry laugh. ***More like bubble-wrapped brat.***

On second thought...

"Hunter, can I ask what happened between the two of you?"

His lips knot up as he looks straight ahead. "Sure. I was working my second year as a licensed pharmacist about the time Ember and I hit it pretty hot and heavy. We met at a fundraiser for a drug company her father owns. And well, let's just say I couldn't bend over backward enough for her. Actually, I would liken it to twisting myself into a pretzel. Eventually, I couldn't do it anymore." ***I couldn't breathe. I*** *wanted out, and she snapped. She stole the med keys, ransacked the pharmacy, and mixed up enough prescriptions to ensure my license was as good as toilet paper. I'll never be able to undo the damage she's done to me. Years of education gone down the drain, and yet the college loans live on. Thankfully, Ember isn't here anymore to take the wrecking ball to my life. If she knew how I felt about Macy, she'd cut off my head, and most likely other parts of my body as well.*

"Oh wow," I mutter as he nods my way. "I'm sorry about all the twisting." And the fact he lost everything because of that woman.

"It's over now." ***She's dead as a doornail. I saw to that myself.***

My eyes flash his way.

He saw to it himself?

"Hunter?" A dam of words begs to burst from me—all of them accusatory. "Who do you think did this to Ember?" If I've ever tried to hone my telesensual powers before on a single mind, it's now. If Hunter Knox indeed killed Ember, I'm going to use every weapon in my arsenal to pull that information from him.

He takes a quick breath. "I think the obvious answer is your sister." He gives a little wink her way, and Macy giggles like a schoolgirl at the thought. "But in all seriousness, I think they should look into Flint Butler, the guy she was seeing. I mean, sure, he's your standard-issue politician, cheesy smile, loads of promises he can't keep, but the guy's got a dark side."

I nod. "He was there the day of the murder."

"Yes, he was. I saw him myself." He glowers just past me as if he were seeing Flint in the distance. "I tried to warn him about her. Out of the goodness of my heart, I told the guy to run."

Macy leans in. "And what did he say?"

Hunter shrugs. "Not much. Actually, I take that back. He said a lot. He said Ember had the capability to ruin him if he so much as hinted he wasn't happy. He didn't have the cookies to leave her—not in the conventional way. He said he had an alternate plan."

Georgie gasps. "An alternate plan? The butler did it!"

All three cats belt out a meow of agreement, and it sounds like an adorable choir.

Macy motions for him to continue. "What was the alternate plan?" *I'm not dating a killer, am I?*

I frown over at her. For all she knows, she could be dating *two* potential killers.

Hunter blows out a breath. "I don't know. I showed up that day to tell Ember to loosen her claws off my life. We hadn't been together in months, and she was still causing problems for me with the board. Flint tried to keep me away from her. He said he didn't want to upset her. Can't blame him. I'm sure he bore the brunt of her wrath."

The tractor takes a turn as we head back in the direction we started, and a tiny bout of panic infiltrates me.

Flint Butler is definitely on my list of people to speak with, but I've got Hunter here now and I can't waste a single second.

"I guess Willow is closing the shop," I say, hoping to bait him. "She says it was never her dream."

He furrows his brows. "Not a surprise. I don't know Willow that well. She seems nice enough. But as soon as I saw Ember and that poor girl looking like carbon copies of one another, I knew something was up. There was a new toy in town."

Macy cocks her head his way. "Meaning?"

"Meaning she probably had something over her to make her jump through hoops. Ember didn't have any real friends. She either bought the people in her life or she threatened them to stay put."

That conversation I had with Marigold comes to mind. Willow was running from the law and Ember knew it. And from the looks of it, Ember didn't hesitate turning her into a toy just like Hunter suggested.

Hunter settles the sleeping kittens on his lap while slinging an arm around my sister's shoulders.

"I'm not sure who's mourning Ember," he says. "And that alone makes me feel bad for her. She may have swept through my life like a hurricane, but I'm sure it didn't feel all that great being her either. And again, she didn't have a mother."

Macy sniffs back her emotions. "I never thought of it that way. I'm sure Ember was looking to fill a void in her life her father couldn't give her. I don't know how I would have turned out without my mother."

Georgie sways toward my sister. "You'd be a killer in that scenario—a serial killer. In fact, you might just have been the first female serial killer in all of Maine."

"Oh, come on, Georgie." Macy lifts a shoulder. "You think too highly of me. Besides, I'm pretty sure our great state has already achieved that status. And if not, I'd gladly fill those killer stilettos. Someone's got to step up to the plate in the name of womankind."

Hunter's mouth falls open. *She's kidding, right? Why do I get the feeling I jumped out of the frying pan and into a serial killer fire?*

Macy finally picks up on that look of concern on his face.

"I jest." She nuzzles against him. "I would never slaughter you in your sleep." Her fingers walk up his chest. "I'd make sure you were wide awake for that experience."

A high-pitched laughter trembles from the poor guy.

We're fast approaching the turnstile to disembark and a pinch of panic grips me.

"Her stepmother is staying at the inn," I offer. "Marigold Sweet? I'm sure if you wanted to stop by and offer your condolences, she'd appreciate that."

His lips pull into a line. "Marigold, huh?" He glances to the ever-darkening sky. "You know, she was the one person who seemed to tolerate Ember. I know Ember wasn't crazy about her. Heck, I wouldn't be too thrilled if my dad married someone a year or two older than me. But Marigold never said a cross word to Ember. It's almost as if she took her stepmother gig seriously. And maybe she did?" *Or maybe Ember had her so chained up with blackmail she had no choice but to play along. My money is on that.*

I consider this. "I'd like to think Ember had a genuine relationship with Marigold. She seems like a nice person. And I guess they were family—you sort of have to at least tolerate them, right? Oh, and before I forget, there's a candlelight vigil for Ember next Friday night in front of her shop. Marigold will be there. It's up to you, but it might offer you some closure if you came."

He nods. "I'm sure it would. Maybe I will stop by and offer up my condolences."

Macy glowers my way. ***Way to go, Bizzy. Maybe I should send Jasper to the town beauty queen and ask them to spend a little time together?***

The ride comes to an abrupt stop, and the entire lot of us is safely offloaded.

Sherlock winnows out all the bacon in Georgie's pocket while the kittens cuddle up with Hunter as if they had found their new home.

He looks my way. "How about I babysit these guys for you for a little while? They look too comfortable to leave."

"I don't mind," I'm quick to tell him.

Macy coos, "Come on, I'll buy you a turkey dog and hand-feed it to you." She wraps her arms around him as we say our goodbyes and they take off.

Georgie steps in. "What do you think, Bizzy?"

"I think Macy's found a good one. Unless, of course, he's the killer. And if that's the case, at least she'll have had a good time right up until the very end."

Both Georgie and Fish howl with a laugh.

The icy wind kicks up a notch, forcing us to cinch our wonky quilts tightly around our chests.

A sea of bodies part before us, and both Georgie and I gasp at the very same time. Walking along the midway between the craft booths and the food stands are more than a dozen women all with wonky quilts draped over their shoulders.

"I've hit the big time!" Georgie shouts as Sherlock barks and jumps in her honor.

Georgie grabs Sherlock by the leash, and the two of them run off hooting and hollering.

Fish snuggles in close. **More turkey tacos for us, Bizzy.**

"You said it sister," I say as we head for the food. "Hunter Knox turned out to be a pretty nice guy."

Fish nuzzles her head against my shoulder. **But you know better than to trust a nice guy, don't you, Bizzy?**

"I sure do. I learned that one the hard way."

Fish yowls, **It's time to find out what kind of a person Flint Butler is.**

I nod her way. "He seemed nice enough when I met him. The question would be, is he a very nice killer?"

And that's exactly what I'm about to find out.

9

The Country Cottage Inn has a tendency to be busy at this time of year, but never to the degree it is right now—and never for the reason we're busy right now either.

After we came back from the pumpkin festival last night, Georgie asked if she and her quilting cronies could put a few quilts in the lobby in an effort to try to rack up a few sales. Of course, I said yes. Of course, I had no idea what a marketing force of nature I was dealing with either.

A thicket of bodies is abuzz in the lobby of the inn, milling around the dozens upon dozens of tables set out with what looks to be a never-ending supply of wonky quilts. It's a little after ten in the morning, and it's been a madhouse for the last hour straight. I haven't seen this many souls at the mall the night before Christmas.

A FRIGHTENING FANGS-GIVING

I've been busy checking in a large group of guests since this melee launched, so I haven't had a chance to properly question Georgie on how this innocent quilt sale turned into a bona fide smash and grab frenzy. Emmie has been making the rounds with platters of her apple cider mini donuts, and it's like watching seagulls flock to breadcrumbs each time she comes out.

No sooner do I leave the reception area in Nessa and Grady's hands than I bump into Jordy.

"How did you know to get all of these tables set out?" I shake my head as I marvel at the crowd moving around at a frenetic clip.

Jordy chuckles to himself. "Georgie called me last night and told me she'd be needing as many as I could fill the lobby with. I'll be honest, I put out six when I got here and I've had to triple it in the last half hour. Which reminds me, I need to know what the inn has planned for Thanksgiving so I can map it out."

"We'll host a Thanksgiving Day buffet in the grand dining room for any guests that might be on the grounds. That should be enough."

"What about you? You going to your mom's?"

"I don't know. She burned the turkey last year and vowed that was the last time she was going to have a date with Tom at four in the morning only to be disappointed in him. Jasper's mother is on another cruise with my dad. I have no idea if they'll be back for the big day. How about you guys?"

He shrugs. "My parents are in the middle of a remodel. I'm sure we'll figure something out. I'll talk to Emmie." He starts to take off. "If you're looking for Fish, Sherlock, and those kittens, they're all with Georgie. She says they're supercharging sales."

"I have no doubt."

I thread my way through the crowd as dozens upon dozens of women fondle and hold up various wonky quilts in every size and color. And no sooner are they being purchased than a fresh supply of wonky quilts lands on the display tables.

Women are walking around with wonky quilts draped over their shoulders and clasped at the neck with fancy looking brooches—sunflowers, pumpkins, and apples made of colorful rhinestones—and the visual of a sea of capes is giving off *Night of the Living Dead* vibes to me. But, in their defense, the only way to get around with a heavy quilt draped over your shoulders is with large, lumbering movements. There's nothing dainty or elegant about it. And aside from that curious sight, there are just as many kids ten and under in attendance who have wonky quilts proudly tied around their necks, and they look every bit the superheroes with them on, too.

Once empowered with the apparent supernatural powers that seem to come with one of Georgie's creations, the kids are running around with a fist in the air, charging and bumping into everything in their way. With so many breakable hips in the vicinity it's a recipe for disaster.

I marvel at the amount of wonky fun being had by all. The quilts only seem to be multiplying. How in the world are these women making them so fast?

I bypass a table with my mother at the helm who seems to be immersed in a conversation with a group of women as they examine a quilt she's holding. I'd stop by and say hello, but there's a gray-headed woman laughing like a hyena just beyond her that has the answers I seek to all of my questions.

A group of women is clustered around Georgie's table, and I see Juni in the thick of it handing out wonky quilts as fast as the grabby hands before her can snatch them away. To the right of the booth there's a cluster of children, and nestled inside of their watchful circle are two different wonky quilts set on the floor, both of them small enough to function as a pet bed and both of them occupied with more than one pet.

Fish and the trio of kittens are nestled on a purple and green wonky quilt with a paw print design thrown into the mix, and it's so adorable I can promise you that wonky quilt is coming home with me. Sherlock and Juni's dog, Sprinkles, are lying on another wonky quilt, black and orange with fall leaves and bones, and it's equally as adorable.

"Bizzy Baker Wilder!" Georgie breaks away from the chaos in front of her and trots on over in what looks to be a wonky quilt dress of some kind. It's white, brown, and yellow, and each swath of fabric has a print of pumpkins, turkeys, and pies. It's adorable, but I'm still not sure what I'm looking at.

"Oh no." I moan without meaning to. "Don't tell me you're trading kaftans for wonkier pastures?"

"*Pfft.*" She gives the crowd the side-eye. "Are you kidding? This is what they call in my biz a publicity stunt." She pinches at the fabric and holds it out for me to see. "What do you think? The idea came to me like a lightning bolt at three in the morning once I fell out of bed."

"You fell out of bed?"

"You're focusing on the wrong part of the story. The important part is, I put two quilts together and left some room for my noggin. And once I figured out I needed a place for my hands, I simply cut a couple of slits on the sides and *ta-da*! It's wonky dress couture. And don't you worry your pretty little head off. I'll whip one up for you before Thanksgiving. What the heck, I'll whip up one for you to wear for Christmas, too. Don't say I've never done anything for you, kid." She gives a comical wink.

"Speaking of whipping one up for me, Georgie, how in the world are these quilts blinking into existence? Are they really that easy to make?"

She cranes her neck past me a moment. "I may have given the quilting guild and the folks at the senior center a little monetary incentive to put their wonky quilt making skills into overdrive."

"You're paying them?"

"I'm charging them forty percent of sales to have the privilege to take part in the free donut and wonky quilt spectacular."

I lean in a notch. "Georgie, is this the free donut and wonky quilt spectacular?"

"Now you're catching on. But don't worry, this ends tonight at six. I'll sacrifice a lot of things to line my pockets with spare change, but dinner isn't one of them."

"Good to know." *Six*? Son of a biscuit. I'm not sure what this will cost more, donuts or my sanity.

"Oh, and I need to talk to that Willow Taylor chick." She snaps her fingers my way as she tap-dances back toward her booth. "I want that space she's vacating. I'm telling you, Bizzy. These wonky quilts are going to take me to the next level."

"You mean us," a familiar voice trills from behind as my mother steps up. She shakes her head my way. "I hate to admit it, but this woman has really put us on the get-rich-quick express. Who knew there was such a desperate need for wonky quilts in this world? I've already contacted the landlord who's leasing Suds and Illuminations out. It's the same landlord that

Macy has." She looks to Georgie. "And just FYI, I'm going to use my sharp business acumen and land us a beaut of a lease deal. I didn't make top realtor in all of Cider Cove, three years in a row, for nothing. This girl knows how to sell."

My ear veers toward her in the event I misunderstood her. "You're going into business with Georgie?"

"You mean Georgie is going into business with me." She steps toward the ballroom. "If you'll excuse me, I've got to replenish my merchandise. We can't keep up with the inventory." She tosses her hands in the air with glee as she takes off, and I'd swear I just saw dollar signs light up in her eyes.

I turn back toward the crowd in time to see Macy and Emmie heading this way.

My sister looks smart in a sleek red blazer and matching velvet pants. Add some horns and a pointy tail and she'd out herself as the she-devil she is.

Emmie, however, looks perfectly adorable with a red and black checkered shirt and red fuzzy scarf.

Macy makes a face at the wall of humanity lining up at Georgie's booth.

"What's with the quilt cult?" She all but snarls.

Emmie belts out a laugh and then loses the smile as quickly as it came. "And here I thought it was a donut cult.

Explain yourself, Bizzy. A little warning would have been nice."

"Ditto." My sister nods. "Main Street is empty. There are fliers lining all of Cider Cove that says you've got free eats and cozy blankets to keep you warm by the sea. Way to steal the business of every establishment this side of Vermont. Not a person has set foot in my shop this morning. I just closed up for the day."

"Yikes." I grimace. "The quilt cult will be here until six. Why don't you grab some inventory and I'll have Jordy set you up with a table?"

"Oh hey!" Her eyes round out. "That would be a great idea if I truly cared. I'd much rather have the day off."

Emmie grunts, "You and me both."

I spot a familiar brunette making her way from table to table while poking and prodding at the wares set before her. Marigold has her dark hair in a French twist, and she's wearing high-heeled boots with a plaid wool poncho that looks so expensive I feel as if I owe her money just for ogling it.

"I see someone I want to talk to. I'll be right back." I take a step away then backtrack. "Emmie, what are your plans for Thanksgiving this year?"

She glances to the ceiling. "After frying up enough donuts to feed all of Cider Cove for the parade, then cooking Thanksgiving dinner for the entire inn, my plans are to pass out in the kitchen and hopefully wake up at some point in December."

"Sorry." I wrinkle my nose. "But good to know. Let's celebrate together at the café if I can get Jasper to agree. Hey, maybe I can invite his brothers and sister?"

Macy's lids drop a notch. She does not look amused. "How about your sister? Ever think to ask her?"

"I asked you a few days ago. You said you were dining and ditching before you shopped until you dropped."

"Sometimes it's nice to be asked twice," Macy says a touch too loud just as Marigold appears next to me with a laugh in her mouth.

"I hope I'm not interrupting," she says as she gives a slight wave. "I just wanted to pop in and show off my new wonky quilt." She holds up a lavender and sage quilt in her hand, and I'm suddenly hoping there's another one just like it floating around out there. It's that adorable.

Emmie sighs at the sight. "That's gorgeous. I'd trade you for a donut," she says, holding out the platter in her hand with its quickly diminishing stash of powdered wonders on it.

Marigold laughs. "No can do. This baby is mine. But if you don't mind, I'm going to help myself to a donut anyhow." She pops one into her mouth and moans. "They're just so addictive." Her shoulders freeze up by her ears. "I keep forgetting this is the last thing Ember had that day." She squeezes her eyes shut tight. "But I won't lie"—she snaps up another donut off the platter—"I don't think even that can stop me from eating them." *If anything, it makes me want to double down.*

I make a face at the sorrowful thought.

"How are you doing?" I shrug as if I didn't have a magnifying glass over her mind.

She shakes her head as she swallows down another bite. "I woke up this morning and my makeup bag was dumped all over the bathroom counter. I never leave it that way. I always make sure to have everything back in place and the bag zipped tight once I'm through with it. I think I was visited by Ember again last night."

Emmie pulls her platter back a notch. "As in her *ghost*?"

Marigold is quick to nod. "It's been happening ever since she passed. She swore she would come back if anything happened to her, and now she has. And I have a feeling she's going to make us all pay for her death until the killer is caught."

Macy looks my way with wild eyes. "You get right on that, Bizzy Baker."

"Wilder." Emmie nods. "Don't forget she's just earned her MRS degree."

"Very funny," I say without cracking a smile.

Macy warms herself with her hands. "Strange things have been happening to me all week, too. I had that horrible message scrawled on my window in lipstick. The items in my shop have been knocked over and rearranged. And last night, my lights kept flickering on and off for over an hour." She shakes her head my way. "If I thought Ember Sweet was trying to make my life a living hell while she still had breath in her lungs, it looks as if she's about to kick that up a notch now that she's gone. She's not even giving me the opportunity to have a single nice thought about her now." She takes up two fistfuls of apple cider mini donuts. "I'm going to look at kittens and inhale carbs for the rest of the morning. If you see Jordy, tell him I'll need him to pull out his ghost-busting vacuum. Macy Baker ain't afraid of no ghost. At least that's what I'll keep telling myself," she says as she takes off for the pet menagerie surrounding Georgie.

Emmie steps in. "I'm going to refill this platter, and you'd better pray there's not a ghost in the kitchen or you'll be hearing me scream all the way to Canada." She takes off, and I close my eyes a moment too long.

"I'm so sorry, Bizzy." Marigold grabs at the diamond pendant suspended on a thin gold chain and swishes it back and forth over her neck.

"Please, don't worry about it. What can I do to help with this? Hey? Maybe it's not a ghost. Maybe you're sleepwalking due to all the stress and you just have no recollection of dumping out your makeup bag last night?"

"Maybe." She shrugs. "But I've heard things from Willow, too. And knowing Ember, haunting those she wanted to impart a little vengeance on isn't anything that would surprise me."

Me either at this point, but I think better of voicing my opinion.

"Oh hey"—a thought comes to me—"I ran into Hunter Knox yesterday at the pumpkin festival. My sister is dating him." I shoot Macy a quick look. "He seems like a really nice guy."

Marigold's lips knot up. *He was a nice guy until Ember had her way with him.* "How did he seem?"

"He seemed to be doing well. He thought the sheriff's department should look into Flint."

Her lips fall open. "I hate to say it, but he's right. Flint is your quintessential politician—with a closet full of skeletons and the determination to keep them in there forever. He once told me he'd do anything to ensure his political career stayed intact. And now with Ember gone, I wonder if he's done just that."

"Do you think Flint had it in him to kill his own girlfriend? Judging by the things Hunter said about him, Flint wasn't having an easy time with Ember. But to kill her? That would be the quickest way to tank a political career."

A huff of a laugh pumps from her. "Flint wasn't sticking around Ember because he wanted to. They argued more than they did anything else. Something wasn't right between the two of them." She shrugs. "I guess the sheriff's department will get to the bottom of it soon enough. Here's hoping they make an arrest before Thanksgiving. I'd hate to start the holidays off with a killer out there somewhere." She sighs as she looks out at the crowd. "I couldn't sleep at night if that were the case." *As it stands now, I'm sleeping like a baby. I wonder how Flint is sleeping these days? I bet Laurel is warming his bed. She'll be the end of him right along with Ember. And not a person on this planet will have to lift a finger to make that happen.* "You know"—she looks down at the quilt in her arms—"I think I'll start my holiday shopping right now and pick up a few more of these. You should do the same. It looks like this is the hot ticket item this year."

Wait... Did she say Laurel? I bet that's another one of Flint's side-pieces. Ember should have kicked him to the curb long ago. Revenge isn't a real solution. It only creates more problems, and it might have ended Ember Sweet's life.

Marigold dissolves into the crowd, and I'm about to join in on the wonky fun when a tall, dark, and handsome homicide detective steps up before me.

Jasper flashes his badge my way, those serious gray eyes pinned to mine.

"Seaview County Sheriff's Department. Have you got a permit for this?"

"For the wonky quilt spectacular spectacle?" I take a step in his way, amused.

"For looking hotter than a forest fire. I'm thinking of hauling you in—for your own safety, of course."

Fish flits over and practically jumps right into my arms.

I saw Jasper flash his badge your way. Oh, tell me he's shutting this circus down. I don't care how rich Georgie is professing she'll be.

Sherlock barks as he bolts on over. *He's not shutting the circus down. Georgie is already rich where it counts—with bacon.*

I shrug his way. "They want to know what that flash of the badge meant."

A devilish grin curls in the corner of his lips. "It means I've got a wife I'd like to protect from the masses. I was just on my way to track down Hunter Knox, Ember's ex, and thought I'd take a quick break to see if you wanted to find a creative way to help me spend it." His lids hood a notch because we both know exactly how we'll be spending that break.

"Hunter?" I try to sound surprised at the mention of this name. I may have conveniently forgotten to mention the meet and greet I had with Ember Sweet's ex last night on that hayride. But in my defense, Jasper and I found a creative way to spend last night as well. It involved some of those apple cider mini donuts, and come to think of it, I'll have to steal a platter before we head back for the cottage to replicate that good time.

Jasper leans in, his eyes narrowing over mine. "You beat me to him, didn't you?"

I freeze solid. "I may have." I give a guilty shrug. "But only because Macy was on a hot date with him."

"That makes total sense." He blows out a breath. "Any vital information you'd like to share with me?"

"Oh, yes." My teeth graze over my lip. "But you'll have to get creative if you want to drag it out of me."

Sherlock barks. ***Don't say that, Bizzy. He's got a loaded weapon on him. He knows how to make the bad guys talk. You're not one of the bad guys, Bizzy.***

Fish yowls down at him, ***Oh hush. Can't you see they've got that gleam in their eyes? Jasper is like catnip to her. And Bizzy is essentially a piece of bacon that Jasper can't resist.***

Sherlock spins in a circle. ***Bizzy is bacon?*** He lets out a few sharp barks. ***It's no wonder he can't get enough of her.***

Fish jumps out of my arms. ***Come on, fuzzball. Let's go make sure the kittens haven't escaped. I'm going to demand Bizzy keep them. They're almost as cute as I am.***

A laugh thumps through me as they take off.

"It's just you and me, Detective Wilder."

"Don't make me cuff you in front of all of these people. Walk at a steady clip and I'll follow close behind. One wrong move, and I'll be forced to tackle you to the ground."

"Oh, I'll make that wrong move, all right—as soon as we step into that cottage."

I manage to snag an entire tray of apple cider mini donuts, and Jasper and I end up in our cottage in no time. I set the donuts down and give Jasper's tie a quick tug.

"Clothes off, Detective. You're on my turf now."

A wicked grin twitches on his lips. "Same goes for you. Drop the stitches. This interrogation is about to go under *covers*."

A dark gurgle of a laugh strums from me. "I don't think we're going to make it to the covers."

His brows hitch up a notch. "Are you talking dirty to me?"

"You should try it sometimes. You never know where it may lead."

"Okay." He pulls me in close. "Who's your next suspect?"

A smile cinches in my cheek. "You really do know how to get me going, don't you? Flint Butler. While you lap up my sloppy seconds with Hunter, I'll be biting into fresh investigative meat."

A low growl comes from him. "You're a married woman, Bizzy Baker Wilder. The only person you should be taking a bite out of is standing right here."

"You are still wearing far too many clothes. Lose them and I'll sink my teeth in wherever I see fit."

A dark smile twitches on his lips. "Flint Butler will be front and center at his very first city council meeting tomorrow night at town hall. I'll be there."

"On city business?" I tip my head with curiosity.

"As your date. Don't dig in any deeper without me, Bizzy. The last thing I want is you getting in over your head with a killer."

"Okay." I give a solemn nod.

Jasper and I get right down to business of our own. We lose the stitches and get right to sinking our teeth in all the right places.

And tomorrow night, maybe, just maybe, we'll take a bite out of crime, together.

10

The city council meetings are conducted in council chambers in the aptly named Cider Cove Building just a few blocks from Main Street.

The room is congested with constituents seated in stiff wooden chairs, as the council members sit up front behind long wooden tables on a riser that puts them about four feet higher than the rest of us. An American flag, along with the state flag of Maine, sits behind them. And there's a banner that stretches across the top of the room that reads *Congratulations, Cider Cove, on one hundred wonderful years!*

Jasper and I came out together tonight and he helped me set out platters of the Country Cottage Café's apple cider mini donuts on the refreshment table. The sweet sugared scent of those fresh baked wonders, coupled with the scent of freshly brewed coffee, lights up my senses. And to be truthful, it seems like the only bright spot in this otherwise dull meeting. So far we've discussed the progress on a traffic light, put out a call for volunteers to make up sandbags for the upcoming storm, and discussed the Founders' Day parade route that's to take place on Thanksgiving.

Altogether there are seven council members, four women and three men—one of which is Flint Butler. I'll admit, he's handsome, with his shock of dark hair and easy smile. He's donned a suit that gives the illusion he has the shoulders of a running back, and he's let a few self-deprecating comments fly, much to the delight of the audience. I can't help but note the way the women in the room seem to be ogling him. I guess I can't blame them. He is newly single, albeit by a little more than a week. But then, he doesn't look too broken up about it either.

Jasper gives my hand a squeeze. ***I wonder what dirt Ember Sweet had on the guy to make him stick around like he did?***

I trace my eyes his way with a look that says that's exactly what we're going to find out, or at least I am. I plan on hogging all of the councilman's free time once this little meet-up is over.

A FRIGHTENING FANGS-GIVING

With just five minutes left to spare, a woman who's been moderating the microphone for the townspeople asks if there are any other comments or questions for the board members.

"*Yes!* I've got a comment," a distinctly female voice shouts from the back. "You've got blood on your hands!"

The entire room breaks out into gasps as we turn to see two people holding up a sign that reads those same cryptic words that look as if they were written in blood over butcher paper. They lower the sign a bit, and I see two shockingly familiar faces.

"Georgie and Juni?" I say just as a couple of security guards escort them out of the building.

The meeting is adjourned, and soon bodies are moving all around the room.

"Jasper, please go make sure they're not being arrested." I plead with him, even though I get the feeling he wouldn't mind so much if they were. Honestly, maybe I wouldn't either.

He frowns at the door a moment. "Okay, but don't have any fun without me. That's a direct order."

A dark laugh strums through me. "I only take orders from you in the bedroom." I give a sly wink as we part ways.

Flint Butler makes his way toward the crowd with that elastic smile stretching across his face, and soon he's met with a mob of women. Just as I'm about to admit defeat, I spot a platinum blonde in their midst who's busy elbowing the rest of the women off to the side by way of a body check worthy of a hockey game.

"Oh my goodness." I roll my eyes as I make my way up front for what feels like a night at the council circus take two. "Macy?" I hiss her name without meaning to as she wraps her arms around him as if she were his bodyguard.

My sister's head twitches like that of a cat and her forehead smooths out with amusement once she spots me.

"Bizzy?" She makes a face. ***Good Lord, don't tell me she's here to give Flint the shakedown, too. Can't I have a decent date anymore without my sister showing up trying to prove he's the killer?***

I shake my head her way as if to answer that internal inquisition.

"Hello, Macy," I pant her name out as I manufacture a smile just for the politician at hand. "Fancy seeing you here." I look up at Flint with his wide forehead and squinted eyes that look as if they're giving out a cheesy smile all of their own. "I'm Bizzy Baker Wilder." I hold out my hand his way, and he quickly shakes it. "I think we met the day of the Founders' Day kickoff."

Flint laughs with amusement. "I'm sure we did. You'll have to forgive me. I must have met dozens of people that day."

"You were with Ember Sweet." I study his features for a moment, and his expression sobers a notch. "Actually, she introduced us."

In fact, Ember said something to the effect that he was all hers—and *his* next thought was that he was going to end that not-so-good time, that very day.

A hard moan comes from my sister. **Here we go again. It's like there's no stopping her. She's a force of destructive dating nature.**

Macy blows out a hard breath. "Fine." She blinks a highly contrived smile my way. "You know what?" She tickles Flint's well-shaven cheek a moment. "I'm going to grab us some donuts and coffee while you get to know my sweet little sister a bit better. She runs the local inn." Macy glowers at me. "I'm sure she'll want to pick your brain about something." **And that something just so happens to be murder. As if. Flint couldn't have done it. I'm a better suspect than he is. The guy's entire career depends on living a squeaky clean life. I can just imagine the fun I can have with him behind closed doors. All of that repressed angst is exactly what I'm looking for in my life.** She shoots me a look that could boil water as she takes off.

"I brought the donuts." I shrug. "They're the same apple cider mini donuts that the Country Cottage Inn donated to the

Founders' Day kickoff festival." I grimace as soon as the words slip from my lips because they happen to be the same donuts the killer used as a murder weapon. "We'll be serving them at the concert at the cove this weekend as well. You'll be there, right?"

His affect swings from jovial to morbidly worried as he glances to the refreshment table.

"Donuts?" He winces. ***Those are the same damn donuts Ember was nibbling on before she lost her life. What the hell are they doing here? My God, it really is as if she's haunting me.*** He squeezes his eyes shut a moment. "Thanks for bringing them. They seem to be going fast." ***They were quite delicious if I remember correctly. Ember seemed to think so. I suppose that's the only detail that mattered that day.*** "And the concert you mentioned…" He looks mildly confused for a moment.

"At the cove with Sugar Shack?" I nod. "They're a popular country music band. They sing that song 'Your Arms Feel Like Heaven'. I'm sure you've heard it a million times. You can't go ten steps without listening to it."

His brows dip low. "I've heard it. It was one of Ember's favorites." ***I wish I could forget it. In fact, I wish I could forget her.***

Wow, that's pretty horrible. I get that he was about to call things off with her, but she's gone now. Why would he want to forget her? Unless, of course, what he really wanted to forget was the fact he sent her to the grave.

"There's a candlelight vigil set for next Friday in Ember's honor." I clear my throat. "You know, candles were her passion, or at least they were about to be. The vigil will be held in front of Suds and Illuminations at sunset. It would be wonderful if you could come."

He shakes his head as if refusing the invitation.

"I wouldn't miss it for the world." That cheesy smile of his rubber bands across his face.

"Flint, you knew Ember well. Was there anyone in her life she was having a disagreement with?" *Such as yourself*, I want to add, but I bite my tongue instead.

He rocks back on his heels and takes a breath. **So many people. Where to begin.**

"Hunter, her ex." He shrugs. "But Hunter's a nice guy. She took him down pretty hard, but he wasn't vindictive about it." **Nope. The poor guy was trying to help me get out of that fire-breathing dragon's way before I was burned alive. I should have listened to him the first time. But no, I had to go my own way. I wanted some arm-candy for my photo ops, and in exchange I got**

a viper capable of destroying everything I've worked so hard to get away from.

Get away from?

"I met Hunter." I give my sister the side-eye as she piles donuts high onto a plate. My guess is that Flint has no idea about the Hunter-Macy connection. Lord knows I won't be the one to tell him. "He does seem like a nice guy. He seemed to get along well with my cats."

"Cats?" Flint laughs on Hunter's animal-loving behalf. "Now that he's hit the unemployment line, maybe he's the one that should go into politics? Rumor has it, he likes babies, too."

A warm laugh strums from me.

For as cheesy as Flint seems to be, there's something magnetizing about him.

"Is there anyone else that Ember may have rubbed the wrong way?"

Everyone else, he muses to himself.

"The only other person I saw getting under Ember's skin was Marigold. They were a forced bond to begin with—through marriage. Ember was constantly saying that woman would be the death of her. And who knows, it may have panned out yet. I'm sure the detectives are looking into it. Marigold had quite the colorful life before she became the next Mrs. Sweet."

"Really? What kind of colorful life?"

"I think she was initially hired as his personal assistant while he was still married to the last Mrs. Sweet. He's had quite the collection of wives. It was actually Ember who helped her get the position."

"They were friends?"

"More like acquaintances on the party scene." *My guess is Ember wanted someone new to manipulate and found her victim in Marigold.*

Manipulate for the sake of manipulation? I'm guessing there's more to the story.

He shakes his head. "And, of course, there's Willow Taylor." His mind flits to white noise—a sure sign his thoughts just took a dive for the naughty. If there is one bright spot in this unique ability of mine, it's the fact that I'm blocked from witnessing any depraved indelicate thoughts a person might be having. It's mostly men that I encounter the white noise phenomenon around, which is the equivalent to snow on a television set. And to be truthful, Jordy is the man I see it in most. Usually that happens after a beautiful woman walks past him at the inn. Even though Jordy and I had a short-lived marriage, nothing physical has ever happened between us, and I'm glad to say we came away with our friendship intact after that whole Vegas debacle.

"What about Willow?" I ask. "Hey, you don't think she was capable of poisoning Ember, do you?"

He holds up his hands. "I'll be the last person to accuse anyone of anything." *That's one way to keep my hands clean. Stay out of the drama. And how I wish I had stayed out of the drama with Laurel.*

Who the heck is Laurel? Is that a nickname he had for Ember? Wait a minute. Marigold mentioned Laurel just yesterday, internally at least.

Before another question can brew in my mind, Georgie and Juni appear at my side like the unstoppable hurricanes they are.

"How'd you like the show, Councilman?" Juni asks, looking every bit like the tough chick she is, clad in leather.

"We're the ones with the sign." Georgie gives an enthusiastic nod while wearing one of her wonky quilts over her body like a bathrobe. "And you've got blood on your hands, mister." She gives a wonky wink just as Jasper runs up winded.

Sorry. He wraps an arm around my waist. *I tried to stop them.*

I shrug up at him. I think at this point we both know they're unstoppable.

Flint belts out a belly laugh. "You're my first hecklers." He offers both Juni and Georgie a warm smile. "What is it you're after?" *I would have asked, what makes you think I have blood on my hands? But I'm afraid I know the answer to that. And I very much have blood on my hands.*

I squeeze the life out of Jasper's waist, and my hand accidentally forms around the butt of his gun, causing him to jerk in reflex.

Juni wags a finger at the councilman in front of us. "You're not here to stop free enterprise, are you?"

"Yeah." Georgie shakes a fist at him. "We spoke with the landlord who owns the dirt under Suds and Illuminations, and he said he can't let the poor girl who got stuck with the soapy bag out of the lease. He said to take it up with the city council."

Jasper groans. "I'm afraid there's been a misunderstanding." He glances to Georgie. "The city council has been cooperating with the sheriff's department. They just need an all-clear from me. I'll get on that, Georgie. I can assure you Councilman Butler has nothing to do with it whatsoever." He nods to the councilman in question. "Nice to see you again, Flint. I'm here with my wife." He nods my way. "The inn she runs is taking part in the Founders' Day festivities."

"Ah!" Flint tips his head back. *So my arrest isn't imminent after all.* He chuckles to himself, and oddly it sounds as if it comes out more playful than it does worrisome. "Any word on the case?"

"No." Jasper bears hard into Flint Butler's eyes as if they were having a showdown. "Like I said that first day we met, if you have anything that might help the investigation, I'm just a phone call away."

"You bet." He glances to the crowd. "I think I'd better mingle. I'll see you all at the concert at the cove." He gets two steps away before Macy accosts him with her donuts.

"I see you've escaped my sister's clutches." Macy shoots me a quick look before handing him a donut.

He offers a smile way. "It's always a pleasure," he calls out. *But having Laurel creep back to the forefront of my mind was anything but. And just like Ember, Laurel Crabtree is out of my life—and everyone else's life for good.*

My muscles go rigid as I try to absorb his thoughts.

"What's the matter?" Jasper pulls me in close while Juni and Georgie get busy passing out fliers and shouting *Wonky quilts half off at the concert at the cove!* "Is it Georgie?"

"No." My chest heaves as thoughts of what Flint Butler might be capable of swirl through my mind. "I think I know who the killer is. And I don't think Ember Sweet was their first victim."

11

November ushers in the first inklings of winter. It seems as if fall is always anxious for an early release as the air grows increasingly icy. The sky is dark with purple and red tinged clouds, but thankfully there is no rain in the forecast today. However, there is something ominous and brooding in the air. It's almost as if the weather were in on something I'm not privy to yet.

Jasper and I spent the last few days researching Laurel Crabtree, and for the most part, we found her via a few social media posts that she was included in. Her own social media footprint is nonexistent. We're stumped as to who she is and where she might be. The only thing I know for sure is that she's a pretty brunette, mid-to-late twenties, with light serious eyes and was once somehow linked to Flint Butler.

It's the day of the concert at the cove, and the warm-up band for Sugar Shack already has the crowd shaking what it's got, down on the sand.

Fish and Sherlock are darting around from one end of the cove to the other, and I've got the trio of kittens in a papoose strapped to my chest. I'll admit, they've been warming me nicely.

Jasper had an emergency at the office but said he'd try to be here in plenty of time to see Sugar Shack perform. But Georgie, Juni, and my mother have not been tardy. They showed up in the wee hours of the morning and reserved a space for themselves near the stage. As soon as the first few bodies trickled in, cold, hard cash was being thrust their way in exchange for their wonky quilts. And just like that, those wonky quilts have quickly become a fad that no one at this concert seems able to resist.

The wind is glacial, the crowd is thick, and everyone seems to have a drink in hand, mostly hot apple cider sold at the refreshment table. The free donuts Emmie set out have already disappeared, and she's busy whipping up batch after batch and sending them out in a steady stream.

Thankfully, the town is footing the bill for those, so the inn won't have to worry about going bankrupt by way of donuts. Although, they're so delicious they would have been worth any fiscal challenge they could have brought on.

A FRIGHTENING FANGS-GIVING

The Country Cottage Café is selling both hot and cold meals in a booth we've set up just outside of the café, and there's a long line of people looking to fill their hungry bellies. Jordy is manning the grill, and the air is scented with the barbeque chicken and steak. And every last one of my senses insists I head in that direction, but as fate or my bad luck would have it, Mackenzie is coming my way.

"Mayor Woods." I pull a tight smile as Mack comes at me with her orange wool suit. The jacket is cut to accentuate her figure, and I can see a pair of dark-brown boots peering from her pants. Even though I've come to understand that Mackenzie pushed me into that whiskey barrel all those years ago on a *dare*—from my own brother no less—I still can't help but pin the blame of my telesensual abilities on her smug shoulders. "Nice turnout today."

"It could be better." She sniffs as she looks to the crowd. "But I suppose there's still time." She pokes her finger to my chest. "I just spoke to Jordy. He says the inn is officially haunted. What's with this poltergeist business, Bizzy? The last thing I need is you turning this town into a paranormal ghost hunter circus."

My lips invert a moment. "There's no ghost," I'm quick to offer up the false assurance. "Some books were scattered on the floor in the lending library, and there were handprints on the windows in the spa that look as if they were smeared with blood. It was nothing but childish pranks." Three different guests reported seeing a woman walking the halls in a glowing white gown in the middle of the night, moaning and repeating the words *you'll be sorry*. That was disconcerting, but there's no reason to bring that up to Mackenzie. Jordy set up security cameras this morning, so if there is a ghost, or a living troublemaker, we'll be sure to catch them either way.

"It had better be nothing. You're not permitted for ghosts."

"I didn't realize you were in charge of building and safety for the other side." It would figure Mackenzie wants power in both this life and the next.

"I'm everywhere, Baker."

"Wilder," I correct.

"Whatever." She cranes her neck as she scans the crowd.

"Looking for your next victim?" I smear a smile her way, and she glowers twice as hard.

"What's that supposed to mean? Is that a dig of some sort due to the fact I'm seeing your brother? You don't think we're serious, do you?" *I suppose if she knew I was looking for Elliot, she would change her tune. Although, if she saw me with Elliot, it would also prove her point. Oh, never mind. She's got me all confused and for no good reason. I swear I lose IQ points just standing next to Bizzy Baker, and I don't care if she is married. Who would have thought a nitwit like Bizzy would have beaten me to the altar? And because she wanted to, not because she had to.*

I suck in a breath at the insult.

And who is this Elliot she's looking for—whom she admitted was about to prove my point? Even though that wasn't the point I was getting at. I was making a dig at the fact she liked to suck the blood straight from the necks of her enemies. I've long suspected she sleeps upside down in a closet.

A trio of meows comes from my papoose and all three kittens poke their heads out at once.

Is this the killer? Pumpkin, the one with a pink dot on her nose, twitches her whiskers.

Spice, the one in the middle with extra-long fur on her ears, recoils at the sight of Mackenzie. ***Oh, she's a witch! I'd recognize one anywhere.*** She jerks her head my way. ***Sherlock Bones has been telling us all about her.***

A soft laugh strums from me, and Mack makes a sour face at the trio of cuteness on hand. Figures. Not only is she looking to cheat on my poor brother with some man named Elliot, but she can't stand to be around anything as adorable as these kittens. It probably diminishes her witchy powers if she stagnates too long in their presence.

"What are you mewling at?" she snaps at the three of them.

"Rumor has it, they were wondering if you were a witch."

A dark smile curves on her lips. It doesn't shock me that Mackenzie sees this as a compliment.

Her attention is abruptly hijacked as she stares hard to my left.

There he is. It's go time. I've only got twenty minutes before Huxley shows up. Elliot and I will need to get right down to business.

She starts to take off, and I step in front of her.

"Where are you off to so quickly?" And more importantly, who is this Elliot character?

She takes a moment to glower at me. "Unlike you, I'm off to make sure the townspeople are having a good time." **And boy, am I ever about to have a good time.**

She zips into the crowd, and I've lost her in the tangle of bodies that has congregated out on the sand.

"How do you like that?" I whisper as I give Cookie a quick scratch on the head. "I think Mackenzie Woods might just be two-timing my brother. I always knew they'd be a flash in the pan, but I had no idea this is how it would go down. Poor Hux."

Little Cookie mewls, **Do you think she'll kill him?**

"No, no." I give her a kiss on her furry little forehead. "Not every human has a tendency to commit murder."

A FRIGHTENING FANGS-GIVING

"I'm going to kill you," a female voice declares from behind, and I turn to find Macy chasing Georgie in my direction. Macy looks cozy in a winter white cable knit sweater over jeans. Admiring my sister's wardrobe has long since been a pastime of mine, but her autumn wardrobe in particular has made me crave a shopping spree or two. And, of course, Georgie is wearing a bright orange kaftan with a matching wonky quilt cinched around her neck.

"And I stand corrected," I mutter to the tiny tots nestled against my chest. "What's happening?" I ask just as Georgie grabs ahold of me and uses my body as a shield.

Macy charges forward as Georgie moans directly into my ear.

"Quick, Bizzy, give me a kitten," Georgie says while scooping Pumpkin right out of my papoose while all three kittens yowl for help. "You wouldn't attack a woman holding a kitten, would you, Macy?"

My sister sheds a growl. "Only if I could attack the kitten first."

And on that note, Pumpkin does her best to scramble out of Georgie's hands.

I give up! Pumpkin screeches. ***Oh, put me back in the alley where I'll have to hunt live rats for my meals. Humans are far too brutal for me to handle.***

I make a face. Fish may have told them the horror stories of what might have happened if Sherlock didn't discover them, and oddly, they rather liked the idea of hunting for rats. I can't blame them. They're hardwired to give chase to a rat now and again.

Macy lunges our way and I hold a hand out, separating Macy from the wonky quilt that looks as if it can land a 747.

"What's going on, Macy?" I ask, even though I'm not sure I want to know.

Cookie stands up straight as she lands her front paws over the edge of the papoose.

Macy? Cookie chirps. ***Oh, Pumpkin, you're in so much trouble. Fish told us just last night that Macy makes a meal out of men. If she eats men, you can bet she'll eat a kitten as an appetizer.***

Pumpkin belts out a roar worthy of a lion, and I snatch her back from Georgie and tuck her into the carrier once again.

"Now"—I look to the warring women before me—"do I need to call the sheriff's department to mediate, or should I cut out the middle man and call the men with the big nets?"

"Funny." Macy gives Georgie a sour look. "I just had three men—two of which were missing teeth, one of which had two black eyes—come up to me and ask if my screen name at the Dating Not Waiting website was Macy-gives-chasey. And do you know what I discovered?"

I lean in. "That you'd rather wait and never date again?"

She inches back, looking affronted at the thought. "You really don't know me, do you, Bizzy?"

I motion for her to get on with it. "What did you learn?"

"That *this* one"—she jabs a finger at Georgie and nearly pokes her eye out from over my shoulder—"created a profile at some app for seniors, and apparently men who swear I was very, very interested in them are coming out of the woodwork. And it's all your fault, Georgie!"

Georgie tosses her hands in the air. "How was I supposed to know they all liked country music?"

"Because that was on *your* list of favorite music!" Macy riots over at her.

"Ignore the men, Macy," I tell her. "You have men hitting on you on a daily basis. Georgie, please don't use Macy's picture as your avatar anymore."

"Fine." Georgie pulls her phone out and snaps a picture of me.

"Hey!" I shout as I try to snatch the phone from her, but she holds it out of my grasp.

Macy gives a husky laugh. "It doesn't feel so good now that the profile is on the other face, does it, Bizzy?"

"No, it doesn't," I say as I inadvertently give the kittens a jostle as I try to snatch the phone again to no avail. "Speaking of men, Macy, how are things going between you and Flint?"

Pumpkin sniffs in Macy's direction. ***What happened to Hunter? She didn't eat him, did she?***

Cookie mewls, ***Of course, she did. He was nice and kind. I bet she had him for dessert.***

Macy swings her hips. "Flint and I just so happen to be going out later this evening. He's taking me out on a mystery date that he promised would be out of this world."

"And there you go," Georgie grunts. "See there, kids?" She leans toward the kittens as she says it. "Auntie Macy gets to have all the fun with the men. Ask me how many men have proposed to take me out on a mystery date? Exactly goose egg." She holds her hand up in the shape of an O. "Teach me your ways, Macy. Now that I'm rolling in dough, I'm willing to ante up to become your pupil. I'll cut my hair, dye it blonde, and get a whole new leather wardrobe just to do whatever it takes to land a man like the one you've got."

I snort at the thought. "The one she's got just might be a killer. Macy, what do you know about this guy? He's a councilman, so what? He was two-timing Ember with you. That shows he has a terrible moral compass."

Macy tosses her head back. "I never asked for monogamy."

My mouth falls open. "Macy, you're going to lose him how you got him."

She gives a hard blink. "What part of I hate monogamy don't you understand? I'll probably be the one to introduce him to his next Mrs. Right Now."

Georgie raises her hand. "I volunteer as dating tribute!"

Now it's me groaning. "Macy, have you ever heard him mention a woman by the name of Laurel Crabtree?"

"No." Her lids hood a notch. "I don't know how you and Jasper like to spend your alone time, but we don't mention other men or women."

Georgie shakes her head my way. "Who knew Bizzy would turn out to be the kinkier of the Baker sisters?"

"Oh hush," I say. "Macy, I'm serious. Has he ever mentioned Ember?"

"Why would he mention Ember? We didn't talk about her when she was alive. We certainly don't mention her now that she's gone." *Okay, so I thought it was strange he didn't bring her up the very night she was murdered, but I certainly wasn't going to spoil the mood.*

"Macy! You were with him the night that Ember died?" I don't even bother to hide the fact I just read her mind.

She shrugs it off. "Someone needed to comfort him."

"Men in mourning!" Georgie spikes a finger. "Why didn't I think of that? I bet the cemetery is crawling with men looking to have a good time."

Macy shakes her head. "Try the morgue."

"Would you two quit?" I step in close to my cold-hearted sister. "Macy, I'd watch out for him if I were you. Flint Butler is—"

"Right here!" Her voice climbs an octave as she dives forward and falls right into his arms.

"Ladies." Flint offers both Georgie and me a nod as he wraps an arm around my sister. He's wearing a wool coat with a thick brown knotted scarf and looks happily cozy—as killers who think they're getting away with murder are prone to do.

Sugar Shack is introduced, and the crowd goes wild. Soon the melody of their most popular song filters through the speakers, and suddenly I wish I had Jasper here to sway to the music with.

"Detective Wilder." Flint tips his head up a notch, and I glance back to see the exact man I was hoping would materialize by my side. "Just in time for the concert, I see. Something tells me you always have impeccable timing." Flint sheds an apprehensive smile. **Which reminds me to avoid this man like the plague. And why is he suddenly always around? Is he onto me? Is this about Laurel or Ember?**

A breath hitches in my throat. "Sugar Shack just started," I say with every intention of pulling Jasper off to the side and filling him in on Flint's nefarious and obviously guilty thoughts.

"Actually"—Jasper's brows hover over his pale eyes—"I'm afraid I won't be able to stay for the concert. I'm here on official business. There's been a development in the case. I'm here to make an arrest."

Flint's eyes widen a notch, and his face turns as pale as the sand on the beach.

Jasper nods. "I'm sorry, Macy. You're under arrest for the murder of Ember Sweet."

I knew it! Spice yelps as she does her best to jump out of my papoose.

Cookie lands her paw onto my chest. *Oh, I could have told you she was the killer. Look at those teeth.*

Pumpkin mewls, *The better to eat men with. She's a killer, all right.*

My sister is *not* a killer.

Now to prove it—to these cats—and to my husband, of all people.

12

Macy Baker has been arrested for the murder of Ember Sweet.

Arrested. For the life of me, I can't wrap my head around it. Yesterday, after my own husband all but slapped the cuffs on my sister, utter chaos ensued. Huxley, my mother, and I drove down to the Seaview Sheriff's Department and watched helplessly as they processed my rather furious sibling. Macy put up a fight, and it was nothing short of a riot. They had to put her in restraints, and then when that wasn't enough, they threatened to *mace* her.

My mother was irate—Ree Baker saves her tears for the pillow. She managed to get herself kicked out of the precinct within a half an hour. My brother did his best to keep his legal wits about him, but according to his thoughts—which were many and rampant—he feels as if he's way in over his head.

Poor Hux began doubting his ability to save Macy from the electric chair—yes, he went there. As it turns out, we're waiting for Hux to get the issue of my sister's case before a judge so bail can be set.

As for Jasper, I'm not upset with him as much as I am upset with the situation. I know justice will prevail, even if I have to bring it about myself.

However, life goes on.

The inn is bustling this morning, sans any sign of a wonky quilt takeover.

Grady, Nessa, and I have been working nonstop processing guests who are coming and going. It's not until noon do we even catch a breather.

Fish hops along the creamy marble counter.

If we're done here, I'd like to visit Auntie Macy in the slammer before Jasper has her shipped to Timbuktu.

I bite down on a smile. Fish may have been privy to a small argument Jasper and I had last night. Mostly it was me arguing and Jasper reassuring me that my sister wasn't being shipped off to the aforementioned destination. Georgie was kind enough to take the kittens from me yesterday when all heck broke loose, and they ended up spending the night at her cottage.

Sherlock barks up at Fish. ***It's not permanent. Jasper made that clear.*** His head twitches my way. ***Bizzy, if I may suggest, I think a little bacon could make this all go away.***

"I wish," I whisper as Nessa nods over to me.

"I heard what happened with your sister." Nessa gives a quick glance around before stepping in close. "You must be frantic. But don't worry. The same thing happened to me, remember? And you really saved the day. I have no doubt you'll pull your sister out of the pokey in no time. So who's your next suspect?"

"I think I'm going to circle back to one I've already questioned." I don't dare even whisper Flint Butler's name in a lobby full of people. The man has a seat down at city hall. A rumor like this could spread like wildfire and could land me in court for libel. "I'll need to speak to Marigold first before I go charging in. But if I'm right, there could be an entirely different arrest taking place in just a few hours, and my sister will be back to her ornery self. Not that she's any less ornery now. Has either of you seen her come down for breakfast?"

"Marigold Sweet?" Grady squints at the computer screen in front of him. "She checked out this morning, just a few minutes before you came in." He steps my way with a stern expression. "She wanted to apologize for not thanking you for the room herself, but she said she couldn't stand another minute in this haunted hotel. Her words, not mine. And when I asked her if anything new had happened, she said that her window kept opening and shutting on its own all night. She said she was so afraid she locked herself in the bathroom and fell asleep in the tub."

My hand presses to my chest. "You've got to be kidding me." I give a few quick blinks, unable to process the thought of it actually happening.

Grady nods. "I know. I didn't believe it either—until the guests from the room on either side of hers reported hearing violent thumping all night long. She's been coming in late all week, so I thought maybe that's what the other guests were hearing, but they confirmed the thumping was going on right up until the sun hit the horizon."

Nessa groans. "I'm sorry, Bizzy, but I don't do ghosts. Either you get this place cleared of its supernatural visitors or I'm walking."

"Good Lord, I might just be walking, too." I scoop up my things in haste. "Grady, did Marigold say if she was heading home?"

Fish lets out a yowl. *I bet her husband is back from his trip. If Marigold thinks she's being haunted, I*

doubt she'd want to go back to the big house she was trying to avoid in the first place.

I nod her way because she's most likely right.

Grady thinks about it for a second. "She mentioned something about an inn south of us."

"The Blue Horse Inn!" I belt it out as if I was giving the winning answer on game night. "I have to get out of here," I say, circling around the counter and practically bumping into Emmie while she does her best to pull a tray brimming with apple cider mini donuts out of my way.

"Whoa, where's the fire?" She takes a step back and examines me. "You're off to see another suspect, aren't you?"

"You better believe it. I'm going to do everything I can to pull my sister out of the cell they've got her locked up in. Grady, would you mind watching Fish and Sherlock for me?"

"I'm on it." He mock salutes me. "Half the time I feel as if they're the ones watching me."

Fish belts out a sharp meow. ***Bring back a killer, Bizzy!***

Sherlock jumps side to side. ***Jasper is not going to be happy about this. I distinctly remember him saying to leave this one to him. I'd put some bacon in your pocket if I were you, Bizzy. You might need it just to settle him down if you get caught. That is, if the killer doesn't catch you first.***

"I'll be fine." I give Sherlock a quick pat before stealing a donut from Emmie. "I'll see you all in a bit."

"I'm coming with you." Emmie slaps the platter onto the reception counter.

"Fine," I say. "But let's keep this little adventure to ourselves. Jasper wouldn't be all that thrilled to know I was heading down there. But it's just Marigold. And I have a feeling she might just point us directly to the killer."

Emmie pretends to zip her lip. "It'll be our little secret." She looks back. "Nessa, can you let the kitchen staff know I'll be back in a few hours?"

Nessa shoots me a look. "Fine. Just try not to get yourselves killed. One of these days, Bizzy Baker, you're going to run into some real trouble."

"It's Bizzy Baker *Wilder*," I call out as Emmie and I dash out the front doors of the inn, only to run into Georgie with a pumpkin patchwork wonky quilt strapped to her back and a smaller version strapped to her chest with three fuzzy little cuties peering out at me from inside.

"Where's the fire?" Georgie holds out her hands and staggers from foot to foot.

"South at the Blue Horse Inn," I say, whisking past her. "I have to ask Marigold what she knows about Flint."

Georgie clasps onto the kittens. "Hear that, girls? We're going south, and I bet we're going to catch a killer!"

That would be great. But right about now, I'd settle for catching a clue.

The Blue Horse Inn is located just below Seaview in a sleepy beach town called Willow Bay. The inn has a larger-than-life powder blue stone horse that stands proudly right outside of the establishment. The building is massive in both girth and width, and could easily dwarf the Country Cottage Inn twice over. There's a ritzy fountain just outside its doors, similar to the one my own inn has, but this one is made of gleaming white marble and the bottom tier is so large it could double as a swimming pool.

Emmie, Georgie, and I storm the entrance, and inside it looks stately, with its white polished walls and glossy white floors. It looks more like a swanky hotel you might find in Manhattan rather than a cozy seaside resort, and I'm glad about it, too. I've been meaning to come down and check out the competition. I mean, I've seen pictures of the place online, but there's a sterile air to it only the real deal could provide.

The Blue Horse Inn butts up against the beach and has a dining room attached that overlooks the water. But whereas the Country Cottage Inn has a simple café, they have a full-blown restaurant and bar. The entire inn is geared for another type of clientele entirely, so I've never felt as if we were truly competitive in any respect.

Emmie grunts as she looks to the long steel reception counter.

"Not a complimentary donut in sight." She sniffs.

I shake my head. "It's almost Thanksgiving, and I don't see a single pumpkin, turkey, or cornucopia in sight. I'm guessing it doesn't fit with their color scheme."

Georgie snorts. "And not a single pooch or cool cat here to greet you either." She gives the kittens in her quilted pouch a jostle. "Looks like a BYOK kinda place to me."

Emmie gives her the side-eye. "BYOK?"

"Bring your own kitten," I say. "I've been around Georgie long enough to know how she operates." Mostly.

Georgie hitches her thumb my way. "That's why you're the lead detective of the Seaview Sheriff's Department."

"That would be my husband," I say.

"Yeah, right." Georgie elbows Emmie in the ribs. "The next thing she's going to try to tell us is that *he's* the one that wears the pants in the family."

Emmie cackles right along with Georgie while I make a run for the front desk. Each employee here is wearing a black suit with a red and white dotted bowtie, the only color in this rather monochromatic world.

"Excuse me," I say, getting the attention of a blonde with her hair knotted up at the neck. I get the feeling hair is off-limits for the employees here, too. Maybe for the guests as well. "I'm supposed to be meeting with Marigold Sweet for lunch," I say, crossing my fingers and toes. As much as I don't like even the tiniest lie, I'm hoping to make that lunch date a reality in less than ten minutes. "Do you know where I can find her?"

The blonde's fingers dance across her keyboard as she looks to the computer screen in front of her.

"She is a guest," she says. "I can't tell you which room she's in, but you could try the Marblehead Lounge if you want to find her. It's to your left and toward the water. Enjoy your time at the Blue Horse Inn." She gets right back to tapping away at her keyboard while I lead Georgie and Emmie in the direction she pointed us to.

One of the kittens peering from Georgie's quilt squeaks out a tiny mewl, *Bizzy, since Sherlock Bones isn't here, we've decided it's only fair we have his bacon.*

Another kitten pokes her head out. *Leave her alone, Cookie. Can't you see she's about to nab the killer?* Her little nose twitches. *Ooh, I smell something delicious. I'll have a helping of whatever that is.*

The third one mewls in agreement, and soon they're going off like a choir.

"They're hungry," I say before quickly relaying their message.

"You don't have to ask me twice." Georgie reaches past the quilt draped over her and into the pocket of her kaftan. "It's raining bacon," she says as she sprinkles bits of salted meat over the kittens' heads and they go wild with delight while fighting for it.

Emmie reaches over and snatches a few pieces right out of the air.

"Don't look at me like that, Bizzy," she says. "I'm not above bacon."

"Neither am I." An elastic smile glides across my face as I help myself to a piece.

The three of us come upon the Marblehead Lounge and crane our heads in every direction at once. It's dark inside. Loud rock music rattles our bones and thumps through our chests. The scent of grilled peppers and onions lights up our senses as a waitress walks by with a sizzling order of fajitas—and what I wouldn't do to sink my teeth into that platter right about now. The windows have a dark blue tint to them, giving the place the feeling it's midnight out. The lounge is spacious with the bartender to the left and small tables set out over the expanse. The floor and tables consist of dark-stained wood, and the entire place is nearly at capacity with bodies—each of them already with a drink in hand as they sway to the music.

"Boy, Bizzy"—Georgie shakes her head—"this makes the café look like a greasy truck stop in the middle of nowhere. No wonder vacancies are up. Our guests have headed for bluer pastures."

Emmie nudges me with her elbow. "There she is! She's seated at the bar. What's our cover?"

The music picks up, and Georgie begins to clap wildly.

"Conga line!" She grabs ahold of a stranger, and soon an entire human chain is linked to her as they run around the dance floor screaming *cha cha cha* at the top of their lungs. Every eye in the place is on them, including that of Marigold's.

The brunette does a double take my way, and I waste no time heading in her direction.

"Bizzy?" Her mouth falls open with a dull laugh. "What are you doing all the way out here? I didn't leave anything behind, did I?"

"Just a ghost," I say, falling into the seat next to her, and Emmie takes the one next to me.

"Our crazy friend is here for the entertainment," Emmie says, ticking her head toward the dance floor where those poor kittens are being jostled to the rhythm of Georgie's happy hip tossing.

Marigold belts out a laugh. "Well, at least she knows how to live it up. I'll tell you right now, that's exactly what I hope to be doing at her age. Let's just hope I don't break a hip doing it."

I nod. "Let's hope Georgie doesn't break a hip doing it. So I heard about the ghost incident." I cringe as I say it. "That's pretty scary. I'm sorry you had that experience. And I wish I had a reasonable explanation. The only thing I can think of is maybe one of the shutters outside of the windows came loose?"

"Nope." She shakes her head emphatically as she takes a sip from her fruity drink. "The window was physically rising and falling. I'm telling you I couldn't believe it myself." She shudders just thinking about it.

Marigold is dressed in a black sequin blouse that catches the light every now and again and has a small matching clutch with her that probably costs more than my car. I've never been one to spend big money on purses, but it sure doesn't stop me from admiring them.

The bartender comes by, and both Emmie and I order a virgin strawberry daiquiri.

Georgie swings by with that howling line of humanity behind her and dumps the kittens into my lap.

She bumps her hip to mine. "If the kittens can't take the heat, they must take a seat!" She kicks out her hip and *cha cha chas* her way clear across the room in seconds as the crowd snakes along with her.

Marigold shakes her head at the sight. "I can see why she likes it here. She's Ms. Popular." Her expression melts as she spots the blue-eyed cuties in my lap. "Oh, for goodness' sake, you sweethearts are so cute you should be illegal. Come here," she says, plucking one out of my lap and Emmie takes another. "What are you going to do with them, Bizzy?"

"I'm sure I'll find a good home for them, but until then they'll continue to stay with me. My pets love them. How about you? In the market for a kitten or three?"

She tosses a glance to the ceiling. "I wish. But as soon as I saw them, I knew I couldn't get near them. I'm highly allergic." She makes a face at the one she's holding. "And that's exactly why I need to give you right back." She hands the little cutie pie my way and almost instantly her eyes are watering, and it looks as if she's been sobbing.

"I'm so sorry," I say, quickly handing the tiny furry tots to Emmie. "I didn't realize you were so allergic. I hope Fish didn't bother you back at the inn. Fish is my cat, the one that sits at the reception counter."

She waves it off. "She didn't bother me at all. I'm fine as long as I'm not snuggling with them. And as you just witnessed, sometimes I can't help myself." She snatches up the small square of a napkin under her drink and quickly blows her nose, and Emmie kicks me.

You'd better speed this up, Bizzy, or she's going to have to leave now that we've ignited her allergies. The next thing you know, she'll have a headache.

I straighten at the thought because, of course, Emmie is right.

"Marigold?" I lean her way. "How well did you know Flint Butler?"

She blinks hard at the mention of his name. "Well enough to know he was a two-timer. Can you believe that sleaze put the moves on me?"

"No," I say, mostly in disbelief, although seeing that he was already two-timing Ember with my own sister, this news shouldn't surprise me.

"Yes," she muses. "He's as slimy as they come. I guess his profession is well-suited to him. My mother always said don't trust a politician. She wanted me to marry well, but was wise enough to offer up a few caveats." She giggles while toasting us with her drink.

Emmie leans in. "She sounds wise."

"She was." Marigold takes a long breath. "She passed last year, and the only family I have now is Warner." Her eyes close a moment too long. ***And God knows he won't be here for long. I'm going to be alone.*** She sags in her seat as she looks out at the dance floor. ***With nothing but conga lines***

in my future. And why is that woman wearing a quilt?

I shoot a quick look to Georgie. "Marigold, have you ever heard Flint or Ember mention anyone by the name of Laurel Crabtree?" I know for a fact she has. Now let's see if she's up for playing along.

"Come to think of it, I have." She tips her face toward the ceiling. "I think Ember said it once during one of those epic shouting matches she had with Flint. You know, for a man who is all smiles on the outside, he was sure capable of shooting off some verbal fireworks, if you know what I mean. Ember and Flint had their fair share of blowouts."

Emmie inches in a bit closer. "What were they fighting over?"

"Couldn't have been money." Marigold shakes her head. "Ember was going to be set up for life. Her father's fortune would have all fallen on her." She wrinkles her nose. "Flint said something once about doing anything to keep her from embarrassing him." A wry smile takes over her lips. "Okay, this is what I know, but I sort of feel bad telling you this." She grimaces. "I heard about your sister being arrested yesterday. I wasn't going to bring it up but, since it's out in the open, I want to tell you how sorry I am."

Emmie snorts. "Don't be. We expected this from her eventually." She looks my way. ***How am I doing?***

A little too well, I want to say.

"She's not wrong." I shrug. "Go on." I nod to Marigold.

"Well, it turns out, I heard the name Macy coming from Ember's lips, too. She said something about that witch wasn't about to get away with stealing her life. Her words, not mine. She also mentioned something about turning the tables and giving Macy a taste of her own medicine."

"Turning the tables?"

Marigold gives a sorrowful nod. "Ember had found solid evidence linking your sister to Flint. I'm sorry to be the one to break it to you, but she was seeing Flint behind Ember's back, knowing full well the man was in a relationship. Now don't get me wrong, I know it takes two to tango, but I'd like to think a woman would know better."

My shoulders sag. "I just discovered that myself. And sadly, my sister doesn't seem to know better."

Emmie does her best to wrangle all three kittens into her lap. "I bet that's why Ember opened that knockoff candle shop across from Lather and Light. It was nothing more than a way to show Macy who was boss."

"Wow," I muse. "You got to hand it to Ember. She was a master at revenge. Hey? I bet Ember blackmailed Flint into sticking around after the fact." That explains why he was looking to break up with her that day.

Emmie clutches onto my arm with a death grip. "I bet Ember knew that Flint did away with that Laurel chick!"

Marigold gasps. "He did *away* with her? I knew he was bad, but I had no idea he was dangerous."

"I guess he is," I pant. "I wonder how I could possibly track down anyone who knew that woman."

Marigold shrugs. "I'm sure people aren't that hard to track down these days with the internet and all."

"You'd be surprised," I tell her.

She twists her lips. "Have you thought of asking Flint? I mean, he may not give you a straight answer, but if he did something to another one of his exes, and that's who I'm assuming this is, you might get a visceral reaction from him just by mentioning her name."

"That's not a bad idea," I say.

A husky laugh trembles from Emmie. "Some men's facial expressions are so easy to read, it's almost as if you're reading their minds."

I nod her way. And that's exactly what I plan on doing.

Georgie comes back, red-faced and sweating, and quickly tosses her quilt to the ground before pulling her kaftan off in one fell swoop as well.

"Georgie!" I panic at the sight of her in an old yellowing bra and a pair of white underwear that can double as a parachute. "What are you doing?"

"Relax, Bizzy. I'm just setting the tone for the rest of the night. Besides, people wear less to the beach."

Why does it feel as if I've got an ornery teenager on my hands?

She scoops up my drink and downs half of it before three different men head this way and clamor for her number.

Emmie grabs the quilt and tosses it over Georgie while I fill Marigold in on the impromptu vigil Cider Cove is having for Ember this Friday night.

"That's so nice of you, Bizzy." She clutches at her neck. "Of course, I'll be there." *And that means revisiting the scene of the crime. My God, how I never wanted to go back there.*

"It'll be in the front," I'm quick to reassure her. "You won't have to worry about setting foot in that alley again."

"Thank goodness," she says under her breath. "Good luck tracking down Laurel."

"Thank you," I tell her. "I'm going to need it."

And as fate would have it, I need a bit of luck to pluck Georgie off of that dance floor once again.

All the way back to Cider Cove, Georgie petitions for a bar to be installed at the inn. And she swears on her life that she'll keep her clothes on at the bar if I do. But I assure her it's not happening. Just like the fact my sister isn't going to rot in a prison cell.

Flint Butler has a skeleton in his closet, and it just so happens that her name is Laurel Crabtree.

I'm about to deep dive into the internet and see if I can't rattle that skeleton yet. And if not, come Friday, I might just rattle Flint himself.

Whatever it takes.

That's exactly what I'm going to do to free my sister.

Don't worry, Macy. I'm about to make a grown man cry if I have to just to bust you out of that holding tank. And something tells me, my sister would enjoy that little watery-eyed fact as sure as if she did it herself.

13

The November wind blows the last of the leaves from the already skeletal trees as a crowd amasses along Main Street right in front of Suds and Illuminations. It didn't take long for word to get out, and soon the entire town seems to have poured in to pay their last respects to Ember.

I was going to have Jordy run out and pick up a couple hundred tapered candles for the event, but Willow had stopped by the inn to give me some inventory for the spa and she said she had more than enough candles for the vigil tonight. And as the day grows dim, we collectively illuminate the evening in Ember's honor with the very candles she was set to sell in that store she opened up as a means of vengeance against my sister. It's a sad story all the way around.

The tiny orange twinkle lights strung up over Main Street glitter like a string of citrine stars. Tons of silk maple leaves have been strung around the doorframes and awnings of all the local businesses, and autumn wreaths filled with colorful leaves dot the doorways. The lampposts have been festooned with leaves and pumpkins in preparation for the big Founders' Day parade this Thursday. The high school and the auxiliary leagues are creating floats in every shape and size. And rumor has it, Cider Cove has procured quite a few of those enormous balloons, the kind you see at the Macy's Thanksgiving Day Parade. I have a feeling this is going to be a Thanksgiving to remember.

Our local pastor says a few kind words about Ember, and after a brief moment of silence the crowd begins to disperse, growing livelier by the second.

Jasper had to work late, but he said he would drive straight over and so I stand with Fish and Sherlock off to the side, watching as the crowd begins to mingle. Fish is warm in my arms, and I've got the kittens in my cat stroller. Already about three different women have asked whether I had a boy or a girl in there, so I told them the only thing I could: girls—triplets to be exact. Two of the three women looked as if they were going to pass out on my behalf.

A FRIGHTENING FANGS-GIVING

Fish yowls, ***There's Mayor Woods, Bizzy. She looks shifty to me. I sense she's up to something.*** She lifts a paw, and I look in that direction.

Across the street, right next to the Lather and Light, I spot Mackenzie looking shifty as she keeps her head on swivel. And before I can think to head in her direction—and accuse her of looking to sink her teeth into another male victim—someone steps right up to her, a man no less.

"It looks as if you were right, Fish," I whisper.

Sherlock barks. ***I'd head over there to see what they were saying, but I wouldn't put it past her to kick me.***

Sadly, I wouldn't either. "I'd like to think she wouldn't resort to a foot to the rear, but she definitely wouldn't be showering you with bacon."

The man in question is tall, dark hair with a heavy wool coat, and from this distance, he seems handsome enough to fit the cheating bill. I hold my breath as Mackenzie picks up his hand. It almost looks as if she's studying it and—touching all of his fingers? Boy, I knew she was weird, but this is next level.

Fish mewls. ***What kind of a greeting is that, Bizzy? Is that what humans do before they get to licking?***

It's called kissing. Sherlock barks. ***And I've never seen Jasper or Bizzy shake hands that way.***

"Nor will you. It's weird."

He pulls her into a hard embrace and lands a kiss to her cheek while she laughs at something he's telling her.

I bet that's Elliot, the mystery man she was looking for the other day.

I quickly pull out my phone and snap a half a dozen pictures of them.

Goodbye to you, Mackenzie Woods. I am so relived you are finally out of my brother's life for good. As much as we were starting to get along again, I couldn't shake that nagging feeling in the back of my mind, and now I know why.

Then just as quickly as he showed up, the mystery man stalks off, and she's left shifting from foot to foot again as she glowers into the crowd. She's probably placing a pox on the entire town. Figures.

Well, it's curtains for you, Mayor Woods. And I say good riddance. I can't wait to find a nice girl for Hux to date.

Who am I kidding? I'd be fine with a nice *cobra* so long as it wasn't that viper.

The sound of music coming from a choppy speaker emanates from behind, and I turn to find a horror manifesting as it strides this way. Juni holds a boombox up on her shoulders while my mother and Georgie wheel shopping carts this way laden down with dozens of colorful quilts.

"Oh no." I can't help but moan.

A FRIGHTENING FANGS-GIVING

Georgie cups her hands around her mouth. "Wonky quilts! Come and get your red-hot wonky quilts!"

Emmie tiptoes my way as if she was afraid to be seen by them. Can't say I blame her. I plan on denying any knowledge of those women if it comes down to it.

"Bizzy, do something," she hisses. "They look like a couple of bag ladies."

"They are a couple of bag ladies. Bag ladies in training."

Fish howls, **Make it stop, Bizzy.**

Sherlock belts out a sharp bark. **Quick! Unleash the kittens! The crowd needs to be sidelined with cuteness.**

"It's too late." I shake my head as the three of them walk right down the middle of the street like some awful parade.

Georgie eschews her hands for a bona fide bullhorn this time as she plucks one from her shopping cart. "Buy one wonky quilt, get a double pack of turkey toes for free!"

An entire group of women quickly mobs them as if turkey toes were the very incentive they were holding out for.

"Turkey toes?" Emmie looks as if she might be sick. "Should I ask the obvious?"

"No." I shake my head. "It will never make sense."

I crane my neck into the crowd. "I still don't see Flint."

"He's a politician. They come late and leave early. He's a weasel, but I have faith he'll show," she says, taking Fish from me. "Do you mind? I'm freezing."

"Have at her," I say just as Jasper and Leo step out of the crowd.

"You two look familiar," I tease as Jasper flexes a wry smile.

"I thought I knew you, but now I'm not so sure." He wraps his arms around me and dots a kiss to my lips. "Leo just told me that you and Emmie questioned Marigold Sweet at some dive bar."

A hard frown takes over his face and lets me know exactly what he thinks of my bar crawl.

"What?" I shoot Emmie a quick look. It's not her fault. She didn't know I was taking this investigation in a Jasper-free direction. "It wasn't a dive bar. It was the Marblehead Lounge at the Blue Horse Inn. And besides, not only was I checking out the competition, Georgie had a conga line to tend to."

His brows swoop in. "Why does that make sense to me?"

Leo bucks with a laugh. "Because you've met Georgie." He sobers up quickly as he hooks his arms around Emmie. "Look, I'm not crazy about the fact you went with her. Bizzy isn't looking to exchange recipes with anyone. She's looking for a killer."

Emmie scoffs. "Well, if you've had her cooking, you'd know her recipes were equally as lethal."

I bite down on a laugh, but I can tell Emmie is starting to simmer.

"Don't worry about me, Leo," she snips. "I can take care of myself."

"Oh?" he balks as if he were amused. "Are you bulletproof? Because if that killer thinks you're onto them, things could get deadly fast. Do us both a favor and don't egg Bizzy on. The next time she wants to go after a suspect, call me. I'll go in her place."

"Did you say egg me on?" I blink back with disbelief. "I'll have you know I've scrambled up a killer or two and served them up to the sheriff's department with a side of bacon—and by bacon, I mean justice," I tell him, and Sherlock barks with approval.

"Whoa"—Jasper hooks his gaze to mine—"Leo is right. Look, Bizzy, I told you specifically to stay out of this once your sister was arrested. You're too close to the case. You could point a finger at the wrong person just to land someone other than Macy behind bars. I'm afraid I'm going to have to demand you step back from this."

"You're going to *demand*?" I slide his arms off my waist, and all four cats in the vicinity mewl in a panic.

"I'm sorry, Bizzy." Jasper's eyes glow against the dark clouds clotting up the sky. "But I'm putting my foot down, not only as your husband, but as the law. I'd like for you to live to see our first Christmas, and if you keep running around questioning people, you may not live to see our first Thanksgiving."

An incredulous roar rips through me.

"You think I'm incompetent," I say, jabbing my finger to his chest.

"I didn't say that." His hands ride up by his head as if I just pointed a weapon at him. "I simply want to keep you safe."

"Oh yeah?" I growl over at him. "Well, who's keeping my sister safe?"

Fish looks at something behind me, and her eyes spring as wide as twin dimes.

I think I'm seeing a ghost! she roars so loud all four of us look in that direction.

And for a second, I think I'm seeing a ghost as well.

"Macy?" I shout her name as I give a hard blink. Striding this way, clad in a red suit, and with a look of fiery fury in her eyes, is my feisty sister. My brother is bobbing about ten feet behind her as if he were struggling to keep up, and I have no doubt he is.

"That's right," she growls with all of her pent-up anger pointed straight at my other half. "I'm back." She pokes her own finger against Jasper's chest, and I have a feeling he's going to be mighty sore by the end of the night. "And you, buster, are getting a divorce! Expect to be served with papers, or have papers filed or whatever it is my brother is about to do to dissolve your unholy union from my sister." She bites the air with each word, and Sherlock barks as if he were joining in on her rage.

Hux quickly holds out his hands between Macy and Jasper as if he felt the need to physically separate the two of them.

"Nobody is getting a divorce," Hux announces before leaning my way. "That is, unless you want one. I'm good for unlimited matrimonial dissolutions whenever you need them, Biz, but I'd space 'em out a little better if I were you."

Georgie hops into our circle of fire. "What's this? The two of you are calling it quits already? Aw, shucks." She elbows Jasper in the ribs, and I'd swear I just heard the breath expire from his lungs. "Don't you worry, kid." She points in my direction. "Macy's going to write a book on how-to-catch a man, and we'll both be back in business soon enough." She plucks a bag of candy corn from her pocket. "Have some turkey toes. They always put a smile on my face." She hands them my way before jumping back into the crowd. "Turkey toes! Come and get your red-hot turkey toes!"

I glance to the carts they're pushing and note they're fresh out of quilts. Who would have guessed my mother and Georgie would form an unholy business alliance with head-turning sales volume? I'd better buy stock in Wonky Quilts while we're still on the ground floor.

But first thing's first.

"I'm not getting a divorce," I say loud enough for all interested parties to hear. I'm about to extrapolate when I spot Willow speaking to Marigold in front of Suds and Illuminations. "Now if you'll all excuse me, I have an investigation to conduct."

I dart past Jasper, and soon I'm right in Willow and Marigold's midst.

"Wonderful vigil," I say. "I hope it brought you both some peace." I try my hardest to control my breathing from the quick jaunt over.

Both women nod in agreement, but Willow squints past me as if trying to make something out.

"Is that your sister?" Her jaw becomes unhinged. Her blonde hair is combed to the side, and in this dull light she looks strikingly like Macy whether she intended to or not.

"Yes, she's out on bail," I say. "And it wasn't soon enough."

"Well good for her." Willow cinches her lips. ***But is it good for me? The last thing I need while trying to*** *rebuild my life is the white-hot spotlight of suspicion over me. What if they discover what I'm running from? I'll do time, that's for sure. And if I run now, I might do far more time for a murder I didn't commit. Not that it hadn't crossed my mind. But unless I poisoned those donuts in my sleep, I'm not the one who should be frying for this one. I'm sorry, Macy. I might look an awful lot like you at the moment, but I'm not paying for your sins.*

I take a deep breath as I contemplate her thoughts.

Willow is officially crossed off the suspect list. And I'm not interested in her petty theft. So her secret is safe with me, and with Jasper for that matter, since he's already been apprised.

Marigold postures my way. "Are you okay, Bizzy?" Her hair is slicked back, nice and neat, and she's impeccably dressed for the brisk fall weather. She's wrapped in a gorgeous plaid peacoat, and I want to stop everything and make her tell me where she garnered that wool treasure. Although, if I did track it down, I probably couldn't get over the sticker shock.

"I'm fine." I try to shake out all of the madness this night has already displayed out of my mind. "How are you? Any more of those ghostly happenings?"

Willow gasps hard as she looks to Marigold. "You too?" **Oh, thank God. At least I know it's not just me. And Lord knows Marigold irritated Ember the most.**

Marigold gives a somber nod. "And you?"

A horrible moan escapes Willow. "I think I'm going insane. Every night this week I've heard strange noises, scratches outside my window. And last night I woke to find red sticky liquid oozing all over my living room floor. It turned out to be the cherry vanilla bubble bath we were selling. There was a puddle of it right in front of my door. I thought it was blood. I screamed for an hour at least. I know that was Ember. It was her way of telling me she wasn't happy that I was closing the store."

Marigold nods my way. "She's after us. She wants to control us from the great beyond. She wants us to be afraid of her from the other side as much as she wanted us to fear her in the here and now. Ember is as tenacious in death as she ever was in life." **Not a surprise. A brat in this life and the next.** "Honestly, I think Warner would be proud."

Willow shakes her head as she looks to Marigold. "How is Warner doing?" There is a pained look in her eyes as she asks the question. "Is he any better?"

Marigold stiffens. "His only daughter is dead. He's doing worse than you'll ever imagine." Something across the street catches her eye. "Well, would you look at that?"

Willow and I turn that way to find Flint and Hunter having a rather animated conversation.

Here it is. My moment.

I turn back to the ladies in front of me. "Will I see you both here for the parade on Thanksgiving?"

Willow glances back to her shop. "I'll be here. I struck a deal with the landlord, and I told him I'd be out by the weekend. I've got a lot of cleanup ahead of me. Ember's ghost really did a number in there." A sorrowful laugh strums through her. "Words I never thought I'd say, and yet I'm not all that surprised." *And a parade—how fitting. I couldn't think of a better way to celebrate the fact I won't have to live another moment under Ember Sweet's thumb.*

Marigold takes in a breath. "I'll be here." Her gaze is still pinned on Flint and Hunter across the street. *I need to make sure that rat fries for what he did. And as soon as the sheriff's department untangles the knot of Laurel's disappearance, I'm sure they'll realize they have their man.* "I've always liked a good parade." She shrugs over to Willow. "I'll even help you pack up the store. What can I say? I'm feeling generous."

"That's a great idea," I say. "I'll bring the donuts!" My hand flies to my lips. "That's not what I meant." I cringe as I quickly step away with a wave.

I spot Jasper watching me with his hands shoved deep in his pockets from about thirty feet away. He looks stern and concerned, and yet very, very patient with me.

And I'm glad about that glimmer of patience in him because he's going to have to hold steady a little bit longer. My feet carry me across the street at a quickened clip, and no sooner do I arrive than Flint has moved on to a crowd of women all cheering and clamoring for his attention.

Perfect. I scoff at my own *imperfect* timing.

Hunter is already walking down the street in a determined fashion that lets me know he's taking off, and I jog my way over until I catch up with him.

"Hunter!" I call out, and he turns around, giving me a sweep with his eyes as if trying to place me. His dark blond hair is combed back in smooth waves, and his thick cologne threatens to suffocate me. "It's me, Bizzy Baker Wilder. We met on the hayride. I was the one with the weird quilt."

"Wonky quilt." He snaps his fingers my way. "Those aren't weird at all. I was thinking about picking up a few for Christmas to give to my mother and sisters. I figured they love that kind of stuff." He gives an affable smile, and I instantly like him.

"Can I ask you a question?"

"Anything." He takes a step in close, and I can see Jasper from my peripheral vision heading this way.

Great. Leave it to Jasper to jeopardize my case. He, of all people, should know better.

"Hunter, what do you know about a woman named Laurel Crabtree?" There, I blurted it out in haste because I can feel the lead homicide detective in the case breathing down my neck. Don't get me wrong, I very much want him breathing down my neck in less than a couple hours.

Hunter inches back a notch. *Why in the heck would this woman be asking about Laurel?*

A breath hitches in my throat.

He knows her! He knows Laurel. This could crack everything wide open.

Hunter shakes his head. "I'm sorry. I'm not sure I know who that is." *No use in getting caught in that dragnet, too. It's bad enough I've been taken down to the sheriff's station twice to be quizzed about Ember's untimely demise.*

My mouth falls open as I give an incredulous huff.

Jasper dragged him down *twice* and has yet to tell me?

"Oh, come on, Hunter. You know about Laurel." I'm this close to shaking him. "How did Flint make her disappear?"

A heavy groan comes from him. "Okay, look, I know enough to get me into trouble. Ember came to me once and mentioned the girl." He blows out a deep breath. *There's no way I'm going to tell her Ember swore if anything ever happened to her that Flint would be responsible. That would be tantamount to pinning Ember's murder on him. And not a bone in my body believes he did this.*

I nod. "He could have very well done this."

He inches back once again. "Laurel was—Ember told me a few things when we met up for coffee a few months back."

"You had coffee with her after what she did to you? After she caused you to lose your license?"

"What can I say? I'm a lover, not a fighter. Yes, she utterly destroyed me, but when I bumped into her, she seemed frantic. Out of sorts. I was concerned." **Ember on a good day was harmful to others. Ember on the edge of oblivion was downright dangerous.** "She said Flint was cheating on her. She thought maybe some chick by the name of Laurel Crabtree was back in town. I guess a couple of years ago Flint was an alderman. He had an affair with a summer intern, a high school student by the name of Laurel Crabtree. She was under eighteen. I don't know the details. But according to Ember, there was legal trouble looming, and then all of a sudden the girl was gone."

"As in missing?"

"As in I don't know. But Ember felt strongly that something went very wrong. She said that Flint destroyed

Laurel's life, and now he was trying to destroy hers by way of humiliating her."

Funny. That seemed to be *her* MO.

I nod. "I saw you talking to Flint. You seem as if you're on friendly terms."

He glares in the direction the councilman is currently working the crowd.

"We're not." ***In fact, we're anything but. I've made a deal with the devil, and now I have to hope everything works out the way we planned. And if it doesn't? I'll be the one to roast once again.*** "Goodnight, Bizzy."

My mind spins just trying to make sense of his thoughts.

"Will I see you at the parade? It's the last day of the Founders' Day celebration. We'll have free donuts!"

Ugh.

Again with flaunting the murder weapon in people's faces?

A dark laugh strums through him. "I'll be here." He glances past me once again. ***But only because he will. Flint and I have unfinished business. He owes me for what I've done for him. And if he pays up, I just might come out of this mess on top.***

Jasper steps up as soon as Hunter disappears into the shadows.

"Well, Detective Wilder?" He sheds an easy smile, and all the stress between us seems to up and disappear.

"Let's go home," I say, wrapping my arms around him. "How does some hot cider in front of a roaring fire sound? There's a lot to process tonight."

"Sounds like heaven."

14

As soon as we get back to our cottage, I jump in the shower while Jasper makes some hot cider, and we reconvene on the living room sofa as the fireplace rages.

Fish and Sherlock are playing with the kittens, and every now and again they zoom by in a furry blur.

Jasper wraps his arm around me as we snuggle and munch on a platter of apple cider mini donuts that I swiped from the café kitchen.

"Your hair is wet." He lands a kiss to the top of my head. "Hey? Why wasn't I invited in that shower?"

"Because you gave me the stink eye while I was conducting a rather thorough investigation this evening."

His chest broadens with his next breath. "Just tell me the divorce isn't on the table."

"Eh, that's Macy's deal. I think if you were her husband, she would have already kicked you to the curb by now. But I have a sneaky suspicion she would have at least had the courtesy to tie you up and teach you a lesson first. Matrimonial manners and all. Would you like me to tie you up and teach you a lesson, Detective Wilder?" I bat my lashes up at him, doing my best to flirt.

His chest bounces with a silent chuckle. "I've got the cuffs if you've got the time. What did you glean?"

"Other than the fact I directly disobeyed my husband?"

"Bizzy." Jasper leans his head back a notch, the distinct look of defeat on his face. "You are everything to me. You're my wife. You're going to be the mother of my children one day. I don't want anything to happen to you." His fingers twirl through the hair at the base of my neck. "Look, I know I can't stop you, but if I didn't try and something did happen? I couldn't live with myself. That being said, maybe it's time we look into a weapon for you."

I pull back. "Like a gun?"

"Yes, like a gun. You can use it for self-protection. I trust you with it. And I might feel a little better knowing you'll have it on you since I can't be with you twenty-four seven."

"No way."

"Think about it." He takes a sip of his cider before setting the mug down. So who's still on the suspect list for the murder of Ember Sweet?"

A hard groan comes from me as I lay my head on his shoulder.

"I don't know. There's Willow Taylor. But I don't think she did it. She's wanted for petty theft in another state, and the only thing going through her mind is keeping her nose clean."

Sherlock and Fish stop in their tracks as Sherlock lands by our feet and Fish hops up onto the coffee table next to the donuts.

She belts out a sharp meow. ***Time for the suspect circle!*** she calls out and the trio of cuteness hops over like a bunch of bunny rabbits.

Willow isn't happy with Macy, Pumpkin mewls. ***I think Macy should stay away from the donuts.***

Spice meows in agreement. ***But they look so delicious.***

Macy doesn't stand a chance, Cookie adds.

"They think Macy is toast." I shrug over at my handsome hubby, and he nods.

"She might be. Anything else about Willow?"

"She's closing up shop. She did say—or think—that Ember's death felt like Christmas and her birthday all rolled into one. I think she's just so relieved that she didn't have this woman making her do any and everything on a whim just because she had her by the cookies."

Jasper ticks his head to the side. "I would imagine she is relieved. Who's up next?"

"There's Marigold, I guess. She's married to Warner Sweet, Ember's wealthy father. He's been in Africa, but he may have just gotten back. I'm not sure on that. And both poor Marigold and Willow claim they were visited by Ember's ghost." A mean shiver rides through me. "I'll admit, strange things have been happening at the inn. I just want this all to be over and for everything to go back to the way it was. Of course, it'll never be over for Ember—not in any good way."

"Or the killer." He lands a kiss to my cheek.

"Anyway, Marigold is the one who told me to look into Flint. She said she heard Ember and him arguing about Laurel Crabtree. Which brings me to my next point. I didn't get a chance to speak with my prime suspect, Flint Butler"—I say, giving Jasper's facial scruff a quick scratch—"but I did speak to Hunter Knox."

The kittens all mewl at the very same time.

Pumpkin rears her cute little head. ***Tell me he's not the killer. He seems like such a kind soul.***

I quickly relay it to Jasper. "And I agree with her. Hunter is nice. Honestly, he should be my number one suspect, but he's just so darn likable." I try to scroll through my memory of any and every meet-up I've ever had with Hunter, and my mind sticks on something. "Wait a minute. The day of the murder, I saw Flint and Hunter going at it, but toward the end of their conversation Hunter held his hand out and Flint clasped it. I remember thinking it didn't look like a handshake or a high-five. What if Hunter was giving something to Flint? Like the strychnine that was used to kill to Ember?"

Jasper blows out a breath. "Possible. But why would Hunter team up with Flint to kill her? I would think if one of them had the desire to pull it off, they wouldn't drag anyone else in on it. That would be messy."

"True, but Hunter had some odd thoughts tonight. He said that he and Flint had some unfinished business. That he owed him for what he's done for him. And if Flint paid up, Hunter thought he just might come out of this mess on top."

Jasper closes his eyes a moment. "Okay, so I'd say it's a definite possibility they teamed up."

No! the three kittens mewl like a choir, and I laugh as I shrug up at Jasper.

"The Hunter Knox Fan Club is taking umbrage with the fact." I poke my finger to his chest. "Speaking of taking umbrage with the fact, why didn't you tell me that you called Hunter into questioning twice already? Shouldn't I be privy to this information? What did he say?"

Jasper's lips twitch. "The legal answer is, no, you shouldn't be privy to it. The proper answer as your husband is, I'm sorry." His lips flex in a wry smile.

"You're forgiven. Did you learn anything new?"

"Nothing. Because apparently you need to be a mind reader to crack this case. He's definitely climbing the suspect list."

I nod. "He's right behind Flint." I told Jasper about what Hunter said regarding Laurel on our ride home. "So we know now that Laurel was working on one of Alderman Butler's campaigns, and now she's gone. She was young. Maybe he knocked her up?"

"Maybe." He shrugs. "Or maybe she threatened to expose him and was blackmailing him?"

"I like her more already."

"This new information is going to make tracking her down a heck of a lot easier. I hope."

"I hope so, too." I wrap my arms around him tightly. "I think Flint may have done this. If Ember knew the details of Flint's sexual dealings with an underage girl, this could cost him his entire future political career. I think he had the most to lose."

Sherlock barks. *That's our killer then. I say you lure a confession out of him by way of bacon.*

Fish yowls as she smacks Sherlock on the top of his head with her paw, ***You can't lure a confession out of anyone with bacon.***

You can if you withhold it from them. He barks right back.

I look to Jasper. "Sherlock thinks bacon is the answer."

"It's the answer to a lot of tough questions." Jasper pats the spot next to him on the couch, and Sherlock jumps up. "Maybe I'll try bribing the suspects with bacon. Stranger things have happened." Those silver eyes of his land on mine. "Is it too soon for you to take another shower? If you won't let me join in this time, the least you can do is let me watch."

"Too soon and too late at night. But I believe there's still a lesson I'm supposed to teach you that involves handcuffs."

Jasper scoops me up and takes off for the bedroom.

I teach Jasper one lesson after the other all night long.

And when I finally fall asleep, I dream of Ember Sweet lying in the alleyway with her eyes opened wide as she stares vacantly to the sky.

"Help me, Bizzy. Find my killer." Her head snaps my way, but she's not looking at me. She's looking right at that box filled with three sweet little kittens. *"They hold the key. They know who did this. End this before I end you."*

I wake up with a start and sit straight up.

Why do I feel as if I've just been threatened from the great beyond?

An icy breeze blows in, and I look to find the bedroom window wide open. And just as I'm about to get up and close it—it slams shut all on its own.

My heart pounds against my chest so hard and fierce, it might just pound right through.

Not only do I need to solve this case for the justice Ember deserves, for the freedom of my sister, but I think I just added my own sanity to the list.

Ember Sweet's killer won't have much to be thankful for this Thanksgiving.

I'll make sure of that myself.

15

Thanksgiving Day is one of those holidays that I look forward to all year long just for the food alone.

And even though Emmie and her army of chefs do the cooking for the inn, I always get up early and join them in the kitchen. This morning Emmie and I worked like mad, mass-producing those apple cider mini donuts at an alarming rate. Since I'm more or less a jinx in the kitchen, I handled the postproduction end of it—dusting those mini miracles with powdered sugar. Jordy was helping out, too, and among the three of us, we created a mountain of powdered delights, enough to feed all of Maine straight through the rest of the month.

But it's the thick scent of turkey permeating the air in all of Cider Cove that has done me in. I cannot wait until things settle down and we're right back at the café enjoying a bountiful Thanksgiving dinner. I've invited my mother, my sister, all of Jasper's family, and every member of the staff to have at the buffet that will blissfully take place in just a few hours. And then after we have our fill of turkey, ham, cornbread stuffing, vat-fulls of mashed potatoes and gravy, along with the rest of the fixings, we move on to dessert. We're talking some serious pie business is about to take place. We've got your pumpkin, apple, pecan, and sweet potato pies. Emmie always includes a cream-filled pumpkin roll to the mix, and I plan on having a little of everything. Okay, fine. A *lot* of everything. On a day like today it would be criminal not to.

Jasper and I spent the last few days trying to dig up anything we could find on the mysterious Laurel Crabtree from Connecticut, and we did find several contenders, but all of them were accounted for in other places during that infamous summer. So far it's been nothing but dead ends when it comes to our mystery woman.

Emmie and I just finished loading a truck full of donuts onto the refreshment table. I've got Fish and the kittens strapped to my chest like a bomb—a bomb filled with cuteness, not to mention I've got Sherlock close by on a leash.

The one good thing about having all of these cats so close to me is that they work like mini heaters keeping me warm despite the arctic breeze. And if those dark and brooding clouds overhead have their way, we're going to have some holiday snow coming right up on the horizon—as soon as tonight.

I can't see the parade! Fish does her best to crane her neck every which way.

Sherlock barks up at her, and his amber eyes have the same sparkle to them that they get when he thinks about his favorite salted meat.

Tell her it's not time, Bizzy. But as soon as it starts, I'm making a path straight to the front.

"Don't worry, Fish." I give her a quick pat. "Sherlock has us covered. We won't miss a thing."

The kittens mewl as they do their best to peek out of my new wonky quilt papoose. I'll admit, Georgie hit a home run with this one.

We're back here again, aren't we? Pumpkin muses.

Spice gives a quick look around before sinking back against my chest. ***So long as we don't end up in a cardboard box, I don't care where Bizzy takes us.***

Hear, hear, Cookie mewls while stretching her cute little paws over my chest.

"Oh"—Emmie gives my arm a squeeze as we navigate through the crowd that's gathered along Main Street to see the big parade—"I almost forgot to tell you about the pumpkin cheesecake I made for tonight. I know how much you love cheesecake, so I made it in your honor."

A hard moan comes from me. "You know me well. I'll have a double helping."

She sucks in a quick breath as she looks my way. "Does that mean you're eating for two?"

"No, it means I'm having seconds." I laugh as I take in the sights.

The entire street is congested with bodies as the local high school band plays near the gazebo. Cider Cove shines in all of its fall glory, as heaps of maple leaves outline that overgrown wooden octagon. And there are enough pumpkins sitting on and around it to qualify it as a pumpkin patch.

The crowd sounds cheerful as voices clash with intermittent laughter, and the scent of turkey baking in every oven in the vicinity warms our senses and gets our stomachs growling at the very same time.

Mackenzie Woods steps into the gazebo, and the microphone in her hand gives a squeal.

"Hello, Cider Cove! Happy Thanksgiving!" she shouts, and the crowd goes wild. I spot my brother a few feet away from the gazebo looking up at Mack as if he actually admires her. I wonder how much he would admire her if he knew she was sneaking around behind his back? "I want to thank you all for helping Cider Cove celebrate its one hundredth magical year." The crowd gives another wild cheer. "Enjoy the parade, enjoy the meals you'll be having in just a little bit, and most of all, enjoy your families."

"Huh," Emmie muses. "She almost sounds as if she has a heart."

"*Almost* being the operative word."

"And"—Mackenzie holds up a small plate of the apple cider mini donuts—"I want to give a special thank you to the Country Cottage Inn for providing these delectable treats for us all." The crowd howls with approval while Mack looks directly at my brother and nods. ***See there, Huxley? I didn't say one mean thing about that dump your sister runs.***

I scoff at the thought. "She just called the inn a dump."

Emmie huffs a breath. "Reason three thousand for Huxley to dump her."

"Too bad *you* didn't find my brother all that amazing," I tell her. "You could have spared me from a fate worse than death. But then, if I'm right, and Mack is two-timing him, the nightmare should be over sooner than later. Even if I have to make sure of it myself."

A little girl runs up and hands Mackenzie a bouquet of red and orange balloons, and Mack holds them just outside of the gazebo.

She leans into the mic. "And here's to many more birthdays to come on the horizon! Happy Founders' Day and Happy Thanksgiving. Let the parade commence!" She lets go of the balloons, and the crowd screams with delight as they dot the sky.

The band starts up, and I catch Mackenzie scouring the crowd before she settles on someone to the left. I follow her gaze, only to find the same dark-haired man she was with the other night.

"That's him," I say to Emmie. "That's Elliot, the guy Mack is cheating on my brother with." The marching band moves into the street as the parade begins and effectively blocks our view before Emmie could see him.

"Don't worry, Bizzy. If she's this sloppy, your brother will be a free man before the pies hit the table tonight." Her phone bleats, and she pulls it out. "Shoot. The kitchen needs me. There's a stuffing emergency. Someone added too much liquid to the batch, and they're trying to save it. When Leo shows up, tell him I'll be right back."

She takes off, and I crane my neck as I try to spot either Leo or Jasper.

Jasper said he had some business to tend to at the station but would try to be here before the parade began. And Leo mentioned he would be patrolling the grounds—much the way I am now.

A FRIGHTENING FANGS-GIVING

I spot the door to Suds and Illuminations sitting wide open, and I waste no time in speeding that way.

"Knock, knock," I say as I head into the shop that holds the sweet scent of a vanilla candle. And to my surprise, I see four women I know quite well, each with a broom in hand.

"Mom, Macy, Juni, and Georgie?" A tiny laugh pumps from me at the sight. "Do I want to know what's happening?" The four of them look a bit bedraggled with their hair mussed, their sleeves rolled up, and the look of abject fatigue in their eyes.

Mom shakes her broom in the air while letting out an exasperated groan.

"Happy Thanksgiving, Bizzy. Why couldn't I have taken a page out of your father's book and spent the holiday being catered to on a cruise ship?"

Georgie bumps her hip to my mother's. "Because you'd rather go into business with me."

My mouth falls open. "It's finally happening, huh?"

Georgie pretends to shoot me with her fingers. "You bet your cutie patootie."

Juni stalks over like a zombie. "Need donut now."

"Sorry, Juni." I wince. "I don't have any on me. But I've got kittens."

No sooner do I say the word than Juni excavates Cookie from my brand-new wonky cat carrier.

"This tasty little snack will do." She gets right to nibbling on her cute little ear.

"Hey, Macy." I head over to where she's examining a box full of candles that's packed away and ready to vacate the premises. "Happy Thanksgiving," I say, pulling my sister into a warm embrace.

"That depends." She makes a face. "Are you still married?"

"Very funny. Why are you in enemy territory?"

"I just bought some of Willow's choice inventory for half of what it would have cost me. Ember may have been a vindictive witch, but she sure had good taste."

A framed picture of a bear sniffing a candle falls off the wall and the glass shatters with a horrific bang.

Fish lets out a hair-raising yowl. ***It's the ghost!*** She dives deep into that wonky quilt papoose while both Pumpkin and Spice do their best to use her back as a stepping stool.

Where? Where? Pumpkin all but crawls onto my shoulder to get a better look. ***I want to see it!***

Spice gives her sister's tail a sharp bite. ***You can't see a ghost, that's the point. Everyone knows that. It's an invisible menace, just like whoever killed the poor girl who once owned this place.***

Both Mom and Georgie groan as Sherlock heads that way and sniffs the air as if he, too, were trying to sniff Ember out.

"Sherlock, come back," I tell him. "There's broken glass. You could get hurt."

Georgie pulls a strip of bacon out of her kaftan and tosses it his way. "Hurt yourself with this, kid."

Mom grunts while pulling out a dustpan, "I was hoping to keep that one."

Georgie waves it off. "I'd rather keep the ghost."

Macy shudders. "I want a sexy male ghost. One that really knows how to make me moan in the bedroom." She scowls at the broken picture. "It really does feel as if she's haunting me."

"It's not true," I tell her. "It's either all a big coincidence or there's a perfectly good explanation behind everything. The other night I woke to the window being wide open and then it shut on its own. Jasper later told me that he opened the window because he got hot and forgot to shut it. And the reason it shut itself is because it's an old wooden window—it was nothing more than gravity." I hope.

She squints my way. "Just what are you doing in that bedroom of yours to work that man into a sweaty frenzy?" Her lips pull back with a naughty smile. "Never mind. I guess you could keep him. He sounds as if he's good for some things." She makes a face again before getting back to work.

Marigold and Willow come in through the back, and I head in their direction. Marigold stuns in a thick burgundy sweater that looks luscious to the touch. I swear, no matter what that woman wears, it looks luxurious on her. A matching chiffon scarf floats around her neck, and that, too, looks decidedly expensive.

"Hey, ladies." I give a cheery wave as I make my way over. "How's it going?"

Sherlock barks for her attention, and Willow quickly gives him a scratch that makes his hind leg dance all on its own.

Marigold groans. "There's a reason people hire movers."

Willow laughs as she wipes her forehead down with her arm, and it's only then I notice her hair has been dyed a warm shade of crimson.

"Your hair!" I gasp. "It looks great."

"Thank you." She glances over to Macy. "I figured no one is holding me hostage to be a clone of your sister's anymore."

Hostage *is a much more honest term than any of them realize. Boy, did I learn my lesson. Never tell a living soul what you don't want others to know. My little petty theft secret is safe with me, and that's exactly where it's going to stay.*

It's safe with me as well. I think this is one injustice I'll let play out on its own. Besides, I think Willow has learned her lesson. Or at least I'm hoping she has.

Marigold nods. "Willow and I were just exchanging war stories from the Ember Sweet frontlines. As much as I loved my stepdaughter, she had a way of making others do her bidding." She picks up a box marked *bubble bath*. "I'll take this to your car and be right back." She nods to Willow before making another trip outside.

Flint and his dicey connections to Laurel Crabtree run through my mind.

"Hey, Willow? Have you ever heard Ember mention a woman by the name of Laurel Crabtree?"

She grimaces a moment. "Laurel? Wasn't that some pet name Flint had for one of his concubines?"

"Pet name?" I blink over at her. "As in—a fake identity?"

She belts out a laugh. "That sounds dramatic. It was a nickname of sorts. I think her name was Lauren Comfort. And boy, was she bringing Flint comfort." She rolls her eyes. "Turns out, she lied to the guy. She wasn't eighteen, she was *sixteen*. Let's just say Flint pulled out his wallet and paid her enough in hush money to make her go away."

"What?" I huff at the thought. "Where did she go? I mean, she was sixteen. I'm sure she lived with her parents."

She cocks her head to the ceiling. "I don't know about that. I guess you'd have to ask Flint. Ember was the one who told me all about it. But I'm guessing it's nothing our councilman wants brought to his attention."

"I'm guessing you're right."

She picks up a box and takes off.

Well? Fish touches her paw to my chest. **That's the end of one mystery.**

Sherlock barks. **Not if he killed her.**

I glance out the window and spot a man stopping to look in before moving on, and I recognize that dirty blond hair and affable smile.

I speed out the door in record time, nearly tangling myself on Sherlock's leash.

"Hunter," I shout, and he turns on his heels.

"Hey, Bizzy." He nods as he strides back my way.

Hunter! Pumpkin nearly leaps right out of my wonky sack. **Oh, he's just as dreamy as I remember.**

Spice jumps up and pokes her fuzzy little head his way. **Cuter than ever if you ask me. Oh, can't he hold us, Bizzy?**

The two of them campaign hard for his attention as they mewl his way. The parade is in full force and the crowd cheers as a group of cheerleaders does a little routine while walking along the route.

"Hey, girls." Hunter plucks them both out and gives them a playful snuggle before laughing my way. "My sisters had cats growing up, and I've been a sucker for cute little kittens ever since."

Both Pumpkin and Spice mewl up at him adorably.

I shake my head. "If I didn't know better, I'd think they were smitten with you."

Fish mewls herself, **Oh, they are. It's nothing but Hunter this, Hunter that. At least they're getting their fill of the guy before you haul him in, Bizzy.**

Which brings me to my next point. "Hunter, I hope you don't mind me asking again, but what's your take on Flint Butler?" Here's hoping I get a confession out of him so I can put this case to rest before I indulge in a caloric apocalypse in just a few hours. A little side of justice would make everything taste that much better.

He shakes his head. "I don't have a take on him. He was a louse of a boyfriend to Ember. Not that she didn't deserve one after she trashed everything I worked for. But he's redeemed himself in my eyes as of late." He glances around. "I haven't told anyone this, but Flint is helping me get my license back."

He shrugs as the balloon of a giant cat holding a sunflower floats on by, much to the delight of the crowd. It's at least sixty-feet tall by thirty-feet wide. Sherlock barks up at it as Fish stands straight up to witness the quasi-feline miracle.

"That's great news," I tell him. "Getting your license back would right all the wrongs Ember did to you. How soon will you be back in the pharmacy?"

He shakes his head. "That all depends." ***On how much more Oxycontin I can drum up for him. Turns out, the councilman is convinced he needs it to relax. And lucky for me, I've got a few dicey pharmaceutical contacts. But unfortunately for Flint, and maybe myself, today is the last day on the Hunter-drug-lord express. I've got three pills burning a hole in my pocket, and he's not getting them from me unless he tells me something I want to hear—like the fact he's willing to testify to the board on my behalf in an effort to convince them that nefarious practices took me down the first time. Someone like Flint might actually have the clout to clear this up for me in a day.***

Oxycontin?

Flint is lucky he's still alive. So I guess Hunter wasn't handing off strychnine to Flint the day of the murder. But it was definitely something that could be equally as lethal for the councilman himself.

Hunter gives the kittens back. "Let me know if you have a hard time finding a home for these guys. If so, I'll be there with bells on to pick them up." He ticks his head toward the gazebo. "I came for the free donuts. Oh, and if you see Macy, tell her we're on for tonight. She invited me to Thanksgiving dinner. I'll catch you later, Bizzy."

It would figure that Macy wouldn't let a little murderous detail, such as the fact he might just be the killer, get in the way of inviting him to dinner.

I turn back toward the shop and find the very councilman I was hoping to question staring inside the window of Suds and Illuminations.

Sherlock lets out a growl. *That's the killer, isn't it, Bizzy?*

"I think so," I pant as I head that way.

"Flint Butler," I say as I come upon him, and he turns and offers one of his signature cheesy grins my way. "Bizzy Baker Wilder." *The detective's wife.* The smile melts right off his face with the thought. "I was just peering inside." He nods to the shop. "It's just hard to believe she's really gone."

"I know." I shrug, scowling up at him regardless of whether or not I mean to. "It feels strange, doesn't it? To have someone just up and disappear out of your life?" Come on, Flint. Throw me a bone.

Fish watches him as if he were a giant mouse and she was ready to pounce.

Don't bother beating around the bush, Bizzy, she growls. ***Ask what happened to the girl. Tell him you were related. Tell him anything.***

She might be onto something.

"Funny story!" I say without putting too much thought into it. "I was just wishing my aunt who lives in Connecticut a happy Thanksgiving this morning. The subject of Ember came up and she felt terrible. She asked if Ember was married and I told her that she actually had a very newly elected yet prominent councilman as her boyfriend. She asked if you were handsome and, of course, I said yes."

His chest puffs with pride. "Why, thank you for that."

"But once I mentioned your name, she said she knew you. She said she was one of the volunteers during your run for alderman. She lived right there in your district. Small world. She said you left shortly afterwards, though." I bite down on my lower lip. "She said you always had a pretty girl on your arm, Lauren Chrissy or something."

His eyes spring wide. ***Lauren Comfort.*** "I did." ***He shrugs. Who the hell cares now? Lauren is married to that idiot I paid to make sure he kept her from even remembering me—another intern, who as fate would have it, went to her high school. Ember can't hold that over my head anymore. It's finally done. I'm not going to hold onto it anymore. It was a*** *mistake, and it's over.* "But before I could so much as take her to dinner, she took off with the kicker from the local high school football team. Such is life." *She doesn't need to know about what happened in the backseat of my car. In fact, I never want to think about it again either.*

"That's it?" I ask with a touch of disappointment in my voice.

What's it? Fish hisses.

Did he confess? Pumpkin does her best to growl, and it sounds ridiculously adorable.

"No," I mutter.

"No?" Flint wrinkles his nose as he squints over at me. "No, what?"

"No end in sight to finding Ember's killer." I don't mind one bit that I just said it out loud.

"That's too bad." He ticks his head to the side. "I just saw her father, too. He's a good guy." *He just had no idea how to raise a daughter without turning her into a monster. Ember Sweet was proof that money doesn't solve everything.*

"So he's back from Africa? That's great, I'm sure Marigold is thrilled."

"Africa?" He chuckles. "I'm pretty sure Warner hasn't left the country in the last few years. He's got an entire myriad of medical conditions. Actually, that's how Ember met her previous boyfriend. Turns out, he was the pharmacist her father used back then. That's when Ember was still helping care for her father." ***The day she met him was the last normal day of his life. The same as it was for me, not too much after that.***

"What makes you think that?"

"He's at a private care facility out in Tuck's Harbor. He's been there for some time."

"I could swear Marigold told me he was hunting in Africa."

He chuckles at the thought. "That's Marigold for you. The last thing she wants is to face the truth. She married a man old enough to be her grandfather just to line her bank account."

"You think she's ashamed?" I blink back, amused.

Flint shrugs. "Some people would do anything for money. And if she sticks around for another couple of months, she'll get a big payout. There won't be much shame in that."

"A big payout? From his death?" I cringe as the words stream from me.

"You got that right. And now that Ember is gone, I guess she can rest easy."

"Rest easy?"

He glances to the shop. "You *know*—fighting over the will. Ember always claimed every red cent was going straight to her. Marigold insisted on it to prove she wasn't a gold digger." He waves to the crowd before giving me a pat on the arm. "Have a wonderful Thanksgiving, Bizzy," he says as he takes off.

"Oh no." Could I have missed something so blatantly that was sitting right in front of my face?

The crime scene bounces through my mind. That fingernail Jasper found indeed belonged to my sister. Then there was that half-used cigarette that was discarded not too far from the body. Sassy Slims are still marketed toward women even to this day.

"Hey, girls?" I give Pumpkin and Spice a quick scratch on the head. "That day you were left in the alley, you said a man left you there?"

Oh yes, Pumpkin mewls. ***The woman told him to put us down far away from her. She didn't want to be anywhere near us.***

"I bet she purchased you." My mouth falls open. "Was that woman smoking by any chance?"

Yes. Spice twitches her ear. ***Her mouth was a smoke stack.***

Pumpkin swats her sister on the nose. ***She was a fire-breathing dragon.***

A fire-breathing dragon. I look back to the shop.

A real monster in our midst.

I have a feeling I know who killed Ember—and who happens to be responsible for Ember Sweet's ghost.

16

The parade is going full tilt as a float covered in mums and birdseed passes us by. The float is in the shape of a giant birdfeeder and attached to its every orifice are exotic animatronic birds that bob their heads back and forth as if trying to get their fill. Right behind that, a large balloon of a cute bear holding a picnic basket does its best not to float off into the sky. The wind is beginning to howl, causing a flurry of red and orange leaves to rain down over the crowd like confetti, and the crowd is growing all the more rabid with excitement with every passing moment.

I'd like nothing more than to watch the parade with the rest of the town folk, but there's a killer in our midst, and I need to get Jasper and Leo here quickly. I'm about to pull out my phone when I spot a plume of smoke drifting from the entry to Suds and Illuminations.

There she is. Sherlock lets out a low growl while Fish and the two kittens remaining in my pouch all peer out at the woman before us.

Fish lets out a guttural roar. ***Don't worry, Bizzy. We'll hold her down while you call Jasper.***

I take a quick breath at the sight of her and slip my phone back into my pocket. The last thing I want to do is spook her.

Sherlock whines. ***Why do I get the feeling you're not calling Jasper? Let go of my leash, Bizzy. I'll sniff him out myself.***

But I don't let go. Instead, I stride right up to the suspect in question and shed a forced smile.

"That's terrible for your health." I try to laugh through the words to make it sound light, but it comes out like a judgmental-laced threat.

Marigold Sweet gives a frenetic nod as she blows a stream of white smoke from her nostrils. She gives a quick glance to the cigarette in question—slim, with a pink ring around the filter.

"Don't I know it." She tosses it down and extinguishes it with her shoe.

"I'm sorry, I interrupted you. You didn't have to do that. That's a Sassy Slims," I say as my chest begins to rise and fall from the sudden rush of adrenaline coursing through me. "My mother used to smoke those. The smell of the menthol takes me right back to my childhood." I glance in the shop to see my mother and Georgie each pushing a broom. Juni and Macy are in the back carrying a box out through the rear of the shop. "I remember seeing an unfinished cigarette in the alley the day of the murder." I shrug over at the stunning brunette before me and watch as the smile melts from her face. "I thought it was strange that it was half-finished. Did you get interrupted that day, like you did now?"

Pumpkin lets out a sharp meow. *The man who delivered us interrupted her, Bizzy! She blew out a breath and a horrible storm cloud came right out of her nostrils.*

Spice mewls as if she were terrified, *And she threw something down and stepped on it like she did just now.*

Marigold frowns, but it looks forced. "I'm sorry, Bizzy, what was that?"

"The day of the murder, you had a box of kittens delivered to the alley. And when you saw them arrive, you stomped out your cigarette the same way you did just now."

"What?" She shakes her head at me while her eyes search my face for clues. *How in the world would she know what?* "Were you there? I wasn't having those kittens delivered." ***My God, there's no way she could figure that one out. I used an alias. I paid the man twice what he wanted for them, all in cash.***

Now it's me shaking my head, trying to figure out why a woman who is allergic to cats would want to have a box full of kittens nearby.

That day back at the Marblehead Lounge comes to mind.

"Oh my God"—a dull laugh pumps from me—"the day you touched Fish at the lounge, your eyes immediately teared up. Your face was red and swollen instantly and it looked as if you had been crying."

A flood of relief hits her. "That's right. I'm allergic, remember? There's no reason on earth why I'd be asking for a box full of trouble." She makes a face at the kittens. "No offense."

"But there is a reason," I say. "You needed them that day to help manufacture tears because you knew there wouldn't be any otherwise—not for Ember. In fact, I did see you take a kitten out of the box once the alley was filled with people. You held it to your cheek for just a moment, and soon thereafter it looked as if you were sobbing. But you weren't sobbing. You weren't sorry in the least because you did it. You fed Ember donuts that were laced with strychnine—something you must have easily procured."

A choking sound comes from her as she begins to dart her gaze at the crowd as if looking for the quickest escape.

"How dare you accuse me of killing my own stepdaughter." Her voice shakes as she says it. "Bizzy, you are badly mistaken. You have my word, I would never do that." Her chest begins to heave with her every breath.

"But you did do it, and your word is useless. You said Warner was in Africa, and yet Flint said he's been in Tuck's Harbor all along, convalescing. He said the poor man only has months to live. Which one of you is telling the truth? I'm sure a few simple phone calls can help me determine that."

She blows out a breath as her eyes widen.

"Don't you dare go spewing these lies. I'm going to sue you. There's no proof that I did this to Ember. Why in the world would I want my own stepdaughter dead?"

"Because in a few months when Warner does pass away, your gravy train comes to an end. You said you were fine with Warner leaving his entire estate to Ember—that was your way of proving you weren't a gold digger."

"I did say that." She presses her hand to her chest as she takes a step back toward the crowd. "And I'm not a gold digger. Flint told you that, didn't he? Bizzy, he's the one that poisoned those donuts. I saw him with Ember those last few minutes. You have to believe me. I can testify against him. We can put him away together. He's done something horrible in his past.

He's not as innocent as everyone thinks he is." ***My God, I have to hook her in. This cannot go sideways for me.*** She pulls her purse in close.

"Flint slept with an underage girl during one of his campaigns a few years back," I tell her. "That's hardly a reason to speculate he killed Ember. But then, maybe his motive is just as strong as yours. I suppose that's for a jury to decide. But, nonetheless, you're going to have to head to the sheriff's department. If you're innocent like you say you are, then there won't be any problem for you. We'll find a deputy right now, and you can tell them everything you know about Flint."

She shakes her head in horror. "No. I don't want to go near the sheriff's department." ***Not now, not ever.*** "Not today anyway. It's Thanksgiving, Bizzy. You've probably been up for hours. Your mind is on overdrive, overwhelmed with your responsibilities at the inn. I forgive you for this. I'll head to the sheriff's department first thing in the morning if that makes you feel better. Let's just both enjoy the parade and a good dinner. I won't take this personally." She backs up another notch as she says it.

"I'm sorry, Marigold, but I don't believe you. You're lying now like you've been lying this entire time. In fact, there was no ghost, was there? You were wreaking havoc at the inn all on your own. You weren't afraid of staying alone in that drafty old mansion of yours. Warner hasn't been there in months.

You specifically came to the inn to start chaos, to keep this town on edge, to keep the deputies looking everywhere but where they should have been. You destroyed Suds and Illuminations that night after Ember was killed because you most likely had a key. And once you were done there, you went over to my sister's shop and wrote the word *killer* on her window to create another diversion. You spilled red bubble bath in through the slit in Willow's front door, didn't you? You were set to terrorize because, in a way, you wanted to pin this all on Ember herself, didn't you?"

Her breathing picks up as ripe anger takes over her features.

"Yes," she bites out the word, and Sherlock barks in response to her confession. "I wanted to blame it on Ember because it was all her fault. If she wasn't so stubborn, and hard to get along with—threatening to have me thrown off the grounds as soon as her father bit the big one—I wouldn't have told her to have at the entire estate. I knew I'd get rid of her before that ever happened. And Warner—he grew so sick so fast. It felt as if I only had minutes to get rid of that ridiculous brat. Believe me, I did the world a favor. I did my homework. The strychnine was easy to procure. I have a legion of gardeners. All I had to do was complain of rodents, and soon the grounds were covered with the deadly poison. Ember taunted me right up until the end, but I had the last laugh."

The crowd gasps with delight as a giant balloon of a turkey sails this way, the size of a small building with its happy cartoon smile. Its orange and yellow feathered plumes look stunning juxtaposed against the dark umber sky.

"I'm sorry I had to drag you into this. But you see, I did a little research on Cider Cove—I had to. The shop was going to play a big role in Ember's dramatic exit. I needed to know exactly what I was up against. And it was you I needed, Bizzy. The town's most prolific amateur sleuth. I needed you to throw off the sheriff's department. And when I told you that about Warner, it was my way of testing to see exactly how much you were digging in my direction. I had a lie ready to remedy my faux pas. You played beautifully into my hands"—she pulls a dark metal object out of her purse—"right up until you didn't. I'm sorry, Bizzy, but you're going to have to come with me."

She wraps her scarf around the gun until it's no longer visible, but I can see the barrel as sure as I can see her.

Sherlock gives a hard yank to the leash until it slips right out of my hand. He gives a few snapping barks, right before he jumps onto her side and does his best to knock her off balance.

Run! Fish yowls, but my feet won't move.

"I can't let her get away," I pant in a panic.

She's going to kill you! Pumpkin screeches at the top of her tiny little lungs.

She's going to kill us, Spice counters.

Marigold pulls me in with Herculean strength and jabs the butt of that gun into my back like a spear.

"It will be over in less than a second," she growls.

The music hikes up ten notches as the marching band ushers that oversized turkey right into our midst.

"There are children around," I shout. "You won't do this."

"Test me," she seethes—and I decide to do just that.

I twist around and snatch her by the arms, the gun now pointing directly into my face. My arms grip hers and I barrel us through the crowd, landing us right onto the street. Our bodies twist and turn as we bump into anything in our way and we knock over three of the teenagers holding the strings that leash that floating turkey to the ground. The bird starts to lilt and I snatch up one of the ropes and quickly wrap it around Marigold's body. The crowd gasps as she raises her arms and the scarf drops to the ground, exposing the murderous intentions in her hand.

A flurry of screams ignites as Sherlock bites and nips at her ankles.

She's going to shoot! Fish roars as she leaps out of the pouch and lands right on Marigold's chest.

Then, like a couple of kitty ninjas, both Pumpkin and Spice pounce onto her as well. And as if that wasn't enough,

Cookie comes charging over from the sidewalk. In less than a second, she climbs all the way to the top of Marigold's head and lands her backside over her face. The gun goes flying, and I duck for cover watching as it lands with a thud in the middle of the street. It spins away from us like mad just in time for Leo Granger to land his hand protectively over it.

A body pounces on me from behind, and I glance back to see Jasper's worried face.

"Bizzy!" he shouts at top volume over the screams from the crowd. "Are you okay?"

"I'm fine." My chest heaves as I struggle to catch my next breath. "She did it." I point over to Marigold as she rolls around on the ground, trying to evict the animals from her body. "She confessed to killing Ember. She confessed to everything."

Jasper and Leo quickly pluck her off the ground and whisk her through the crowd.

Sherlock and Fish herd the kittens my way, and I put them all back into my wonky quilt papoose, much to the delight of the crowd. Fish hops into my arms and we finally make our way back to the sidewalk.

Macy runs my way and shakes me.

"I saw the whole thing!" she shouts. "Are you nuts? That woman had a *gun*."

A FRIGHTENING FANGS-GIVING

"You're free." I pull my sister in and give her a firm embrace. "It's all over."

The crowd gives a raucous cheer, and Macy and I turn to see a giant sleigh making its way down the street. Santa sits at the helm while tossing candy canes left and right to anyone willing to catch them.

Macy slings her arm over my shoulders. "That man in the red suit looks luscious. How about I wrap him up with a bow and gift him to you for Christmas? After all you've done for me, you deserve it."

"Macy"—I give her the side-eye for even suggesting it—"I'm a happily married woman."

She makes a face. "So I guess you're sticking with the traitor, huh?"

"He's not a traitor. He was doing his job."

"You did his job for him. But don't tell him I said that. Something tells me, I'd better stay on his good side."

The crowd goes wild, and we look up just in time to see Santa winking at us before it rains candy canes in our direction.

This holiday isn't even over, and it's already passing the baton to the next.

Everything is happening so quickly. But one thing is for sure—everything will taste a little bit better today knowing that justice was served up cold to the woman who killed Ember Sweet.

Rest in peace, Ember.

I glance to her shop just as a pale handprint appears on the storefront window like a plume of fog before slowly evaporating.

Maybe, just maybe, Ember Sweet had the last word after all.

17

Thanksgiving has always meant two things to me: food and family.

I marvel as I look around at the faces who have joined me for this glorious feast. Jasper's three brothers and his sister, Ella, have stopped by—including Ella's husband and their seven-month-old daughter, Willow. Macy, my mother, and Huxley are here. Georgie and Juni, and that guy with the jelly belly Juni picked up at the Happy Hour bar a few weeks back have shown up.

Macy is here with Hunter as her date. My brother had to bring Mackenzie, much to my dismay, and I've been biting my tongue this entire time not wanting to ruin this perfect meal by accusing her of two-timing Huxley. Jordy is here, too, having a lively conversation with Hux at the moment.

Leo and Emmie are canoodling at the other end of the table while everyone finishes up with their meal.

And last but never least, I have Jasper Wilder by my side, handsome and strong and every bit the naughty detective as he flirts merciless with me all through dinner—telepathically, of course.

Fish and Sherlock sit by the fire, along with Emmie and Leo's dogs, Cinnamon, a labradoodle that looks like a bona fide teddy bear, and Gatsby, a handsome golden retriever. Nessa's little dog, Peanut, and Sprinkles, Juni's Yorkie, are here, too. And the kittens are most certainly here. All three of them have enjoyed tumbling around with the dogs while Fish does her best to mind them like a mama bear, or in this case, a mama *cat*.

It turned out, not a single guest was here to have dinner at the inn. Each of them went off to celebrate with family in the area. I tried sending both Grady and Nessa home early, but after they insisted on helping every last guest, *I* insisted they have a bite to eat with us before they left. And they both happily complied.

Since the grand dining room would be empty, and the buffet gone to waste, we moved our private party into this room. It's a far more fancier setting than pulling a few tables together in the café.

A FRIGHTENING FANGS-GIVING

The fireplace is roaring, and the wood paneled walls are decorated with swags of maple leaves. The expansive table is dotted with pumpkins all the way across, and sitting in the very middle is a cornucopia brimming with gourds and corn. But the real showstopper is the food the Country Cottage Café provided. A smorgasbord of every offering this holiday requires, including three different turkeys cooked three different ways—smoked, roasted, and fried. And suffice it to say, I ate more than my fair share of each.

Grady comes over while slipping on his jacket. "I'll see you tomorrow, Bizzy."

Nessa rises from the table as well. "Thanks for having us. My mother is going to kill me when I show up to her house with a full belly."

Emmie stands. "I'll walk you out. I've got pies that need to be brought over from the café."

Jordy jumps up. "I'll help. The sooner they get here, the sooner they get in my stomach."

Soon, the entire room is on their feet as if this were the seventh inning stretch. Because, let's face it, we all know this meal is far from over.

Jasper bows in and lands a kiss to my cheek. "Dinner was wonderful. You're wonderful." He brushes the hair from my eyes. "You did it. You solved another case. November may have been a whirlwind, but I predict we're going to have a calm and peaceful December. It's Christmastime, it's practically a requirement." He hitches his head toward the crowd to our left. "Let's head over to my brother's. I think they're eyeing your mother with less than chaste intent."

A laugh bumps from me. "It wouldn't be the first time," I say just as Macy and Hunter step this way. "I'll be right there."

Jasper takes off just as Macy offers me a hug.

"It's been real." She pulls back with tears in her eyes. "Thanks for facing a gun-toting madwoman just to clear my name. I would like to think I'd do the same for you." She shrugs. "I most likely wouldn't, but you never know."

The three of us share a laugh as the kittens run over and practically claw their way up Hunter's pants.

"Whoa." He quickly scoops them up into his arms. "I don't think I can get enough of this cuteness." He dots a quick kiss to each of their foreheads.

Georgie strides up with Fish in her arms. "Looks like the terrific trio has finally found a home." She slaps Hunter on his back. "It was fate, kid. Stop by my new shop and I'll set you up with a wonky quilt these cool cats can call their own. They were destined to be yours. Sometimes we choose the sweet treat, and sometimes the sweet treat chooses us."

Macy shakes her head. "That's too much dessert for one person."

Hunter shrugs as he looks my way. "I don't know, I think I can handle it. What do you think, Bizzy? Can I be the good home these girls need and deserve?"

All three of the kittens mewl in turn, begging and pleading with me to let it be so.

Fish sighs. ***Go ahead and do it, Bizzy. But only if we can see them again.***

I take a deep breath. "Then let it be so, indeed. Congratulations, Hunter. You're the father to three baby girls. And I have no doubt you'll take good care of them. Just be sure to visit the inn with them again. We're going to miss them like crazy."

Macy sighs his way. "I don't suppose you'll have room for one more girl in your life, would you?"

He chuckles at the thought. "For you, kitten, there's always room."

Georgie leads them to the fireplace as she formally introduces Hunter to the rest of the menagerie while the furry cutie pies do their best to lick his face clean.

I'm about to head over to Jasper when Leo steps in front of me.

He looks handsome in a casual jacket with a dress shirt on underneath. And judging by those rampant heated thoughts Emmie was having all through dinner, Emmie more than noticed just how handsome he looks.

"I hope you don't mind." He shifts from foot to foot while giving an apprehensive smile. "I've got a huge favor to ask."

"Anything," I say as I lean in. "Leo, we're family, and not because we're both telesensual. Emmie is head over heels in love with you."

He takes a breath. "That's exactly how I feel about her." He nods. "I'm going to do it. I'm going to pop the question on Christmas Eve, Bizzy."

My mouth falls open, and I take in a never-ending breath.

He gives a nervous laugh. "I want you to help me figure out the perfect proposal, and I want you to help me pick out the perfect ring, too. I need this to be special, and nobody knows Emmie the way you do. Will you do it? Will you help?"

I toss my arms around him and give him a hard embrace as I sniff back tears. "You bet I will. I'll get my wheels turning right away. Don't you worry. Emmie Crosby is going to have the world's most perfect proposal. Everything is going to be special. Thank you, Leo, for loving her the way you do. She's lucky to have you."

"I'm the lucky one." He nods to someone from over my shoulder. "I'd better tell Jasper."

I'm about to go with him when Huxley cuts me off at the pass.

"Hey, Biz, got a second?" He scratches at the back of his neck, a sure sign he's nervous—and considering whom he's with, I don't blame him. Mackenzie probably has the power to make even her own *mother* twitchy.

"Of course, what do you need? An escape route?"

He shoots me a look. "All right, you're very funny. I know that was a dig at Mack, but I want you to like her. In fact, I want you to *love* her. If I get my way, she's going to be around for a very long time. I'm going to ask her to marry me, come Christmas Eve." He blows out a heavy sigh. "And I want you to help me plan it."

A hard groan comes from me, the kind that expels from you by way of a good sock to the stomach.

"Of course," I hear myself say. I couldn't deny my brother anything, least of all his delusions.

"Great." He perks up a notch. "I'll need help with the ring, too. Nothing too flashy. Underneath it all, Mackenzie is a simple girl."

More like simple cheater.

"Fine. I'll help pick out the ring, but nothing pointy that can be used against you later as a weapon."

He bucks with a laugh. "You're killing me."

I want to say *let's hope Mackenzie doesn't kill you first*, but I opt to glue my lips shut instead.

He pats me on the back. "I need some more of that cider. Are you up for a cup?"

"No thanks," I say as he takes off. As much as I want to join Jasper and his family, I'm afraid I'm needed elsewhere. I winnow Mackenzie out from a conversation she seems to be having with Juni, and I pull her to the side.

"I know what you're up to," I hiss. Mackenzie's wild chestnut hair cascades down her back, and she's wearing a cranberry pantsuit with matching heels, looking every bit the devil she is. "If you have any decency at all, you'll break it off with my brother as soon as this party is over. I don't appreciate you using him like your plaything."

She squints hard over at me. "What are you warbling about? And what's so bad about your brother being my plaything? I, for one, happen to know he enjoys it."

"Gross," I grunt as I pull out my phone and quickly riffle through my pictures until I come across the bomb that's about to blow the lid off of Mackenzie's cheating ways. "We both know you're two-timing my brother, and you're doing it with this man right here." I shove the phone to her face, and her mouth squares out as she examines the picture.

"What in the hell?" She shakes her head as she steps back. "Are you following me?"

"I didn't have to. You did that out in the open. And don't play Ms. Innocent with me. I could practically read your mind that day. You didn't want Huxley to see you."

She cranes her neck past my shoulder for a moment. "Fine. You're right," she snips in my face. "I didn't want Hux to see us together. That's Elliot Timber, my *cousin* who happens to work at a jewelry store in Rose Glen. If you must know my business, I'm getting ready to propose to your brother."

"*What?*" I squawk so loud the room quiets down to a hush before picking up once again with its pleasant din. "You're going to *propose?*"

"Would you keep it down before you ruin everything? And yes." She practically bites my nose off when she says it. "I'm going to propose, and I want you to help. I need you to get his class ring or something. I want the ring to fit when I give it to him."

"Class ring?" I ask, stunned. "Fine." I close my eyes in defeat. "I'll ask my mother. I think it's actually in her possession."

"Never mind, I can ask her myself." Her lips curl at the tips. "And once your brother says yes, on Christmas Eve, you'll have a brand-new sister to look forward to—me." She gives a malevolent wink. "I've always felt a connection to you, Bizzy. Something extra besides the friendship we once shared, and now I know why. It was destiny that we become family all along." Her shoulders bounce. "Be warned, if you ruin my surprise, I'll make you pay." She stalks off, and I sag at the thought of being permanently leashed to Mackenzie Woods as family.

Before I can process any of it, Emmie and Jordy wheel in a couple of carts laden down with enough pumpkin, pecan, and apple pies to feed a small island nation—not to mention a mound of those apple cider mini donuts. And I think I see a pumpkin cheesecake on there, too.

Jasper comes up. "Here you are. I was getting worried." He bears those lightning gray eyes to mine. "Is everything okay?"

I'm about to answer when Grady pokes his head back into the room and heads this way.

"I was about to take off when I spotted this on the desk. It must have come in with yesterday's mail. Sorry, things were a bit frantic. Happy Thanksgiving," he says as hands me a white envelope with the word *urgent* written on the back and the return address is a quite a familiar one.

"It's from Quinn Bennet, the owner of the inn," I say as I open it up, and both Jasper and I quickly read it.

Dear Bizzy,

I hope this letter finds you well. I'm headed stateside on business, and while I'm in town, I'll be entertaining a few of my closest friends. They are an interesting group, I'm sure you'll adore them. Have the inn ready for a grand holiday party on the first Saturday of December. This is going to be a holiday season to remember.

Warmly,

Earl Quinn Bennet

I close my eyes for a moment before looking up at my handsome husband. "So much for a peaceful holiday season."

He wraps his arms around me. "I have a feeling this will be a Christmas to remember, indeed."

I nod up at him. "It will be."

I can feel it in my creaky bones.

The inn is about to host the party of the year, and I have less than a week to put it all together.

Two proposals and one very potent party are coming right up.

Here's hoping I survive them all.

And if the murderous track record this town holds is any indication, someone may not survive at all.

Recipe

Country Cottage Café
Apple Cider Donuts

Hey all! Bizzy here saying hello! We're still enjoying fall here in Cider Cove in all its crisp air, colorful leaves, and roaring fire glory. The Country Cottage Café has the best recipe for cool fall nights, and we hope you'll enjoy these sweet treats as much as we have. Happy baking!

Ingredients

1 ¾ cup all-purpose flour
1 ¼ teaspoon baking powder
¾ teaspoon salt
2 teaspoons ground cinnamon *total* (1 teaspoon cinnamon for batter. 1 teaspoon cinnamon for topping.)
½ teaspoon nutmeg (freshly grated works great, too)
1 cup unsalted butter, room temperature *total* (10 tablespoons of butter for batter. 6 tablespoons of butter to brush over donuts before dredging with sugar and cinnamon once they're baked.)

¾ cup light brown sugar

¾ cup granulated sugar *total* (¼ cup granulated sugar for batter. ½ cup granulated sugar will be saved for topping.)

2 large eggs, room temperature

1 teaspoon vanilla extract

½ cup apple cider

Directions

Preheat oven to 350°.

Grease 2 donut pans with nonstick spray.

In a large bowl, add the flour, baking powder, salt, 1 teaspoon cinnamon, and nutmeg.

In a stand mixer, use the paddle attachment and cream 10 tablespoons butter, brown sugar, and 1/4 cup granulated sugar on medium until light and fluffy. Add the eggs and blend, scraping the bowl as needed. Add in vanilla extract. Add flour and mix on low until well combined. Slowly add apple cider.

Spoon or pipe batter into the donut pan, filling 2/3 of the way full. Bake 12 minutes or until golden brown, and a toothpick inserted into the center comes out clean.

Once donuts are baked, the fun begins! Get ready to roll in all the yummy goodness of sugar and cinnamon.

*In a small bowl, combine remaining 1/2 cup granulated sugar and 1 teaspoon cinnamon. In another small bowl, melt the remaining 6 tablespoons of butter in the microwave. Once donuts have cooled, brush with the butter and dip them into the cinnamon sugar mixture.

Serve and enjoy!

A Note from the Authors

Look for **A Christmas to Dismember (Country Cottage Mysteries 12)** coming up next!

Thank you for reading **A Frightening Fangs-giving (Country Cottage Mysteries 11).**

Acknowledgements

Thank YOU, the reader, for joining us on this adventure to Cider Cove. We hope you're enjoying the Country Cottage Mysteries as much as we are. Don't miss A Christmas to Dismember coming up next. It's Christmas in Cider Cover! Thank you so much from the bottom of our hearts for taking this journey with us. We cannot wait to take you back to Cider Cove!

Special thank you to the following people for taking care of this book—Kaila Eileen Turingan-Ramos, Jodie Tarleton, Margaret Lapointe, and Lisa Markson. And a very big shout out to Lou Harper of Cover Affairs for designing the world's best covers.

A heartfelt thank you to Paige Maroney Smith for being so amazing in every single way.

And last, but never least, thank you to Him who sits on the throne. Worthy is the Lamb! Glory and honor and power are yours. We owe you everything.

About the Author

Bellamy Bloom

Bellamy Bloom is a **USA TODAY** bestselling author who writes cozy mysteries filled with humor, intrigue and a touch of the supernatural. When she's not writing up a murderous storm she's snuggled by the fire with her two precious pooches, chewing down her to-be-read pile and drinking copious amounts of coffee.

Visit her at:

www.authorbellamybloom.com

Addison Moore

Addison Moore is a **New York Times**, **USA TODAY** and **Wall Street Journal** bestselling author who writes mystery, psychological thrillers and romance. Her work has been featured in ***Cosmopolitan*** Magazine. Previously she worked as a therapist on a locked psychiatric unit for nearly a decade. She resides on the West Coast with her husband, four wonderful children, and two dogs where eats too much chocolate and stays up way too late. When she's not writing, she's reading. Addison's Celestra Series has been optioned for film by **20th Century Fox.**

Feel free to visit her at:

www.addisonmoore.com

Made in the USA
Las Vegas, NV
26 April 2022